Will You Be My Wi-Fi?

Also by Caroline Linden

The Wagers of Sin
My Once and Future Duke
An Earl Like You
When the Marquess Was Mine

The Scandals Series
Love and Other Scandals
All's Fair in Love and Scandal (novella)
It Takes a Scandal
Love in the Time of Scandal
A Study in Scandal (novella)
Six Degrees of Scandal
The Secret of My Seduction (novella)

The Truth About the Duke
I Love the Earl (novella)
One Night in London
Blame It on Bath
The Way to a Duke's Heart

The Reece Trilogy
What a Gentleman Wants
What a Rogue Desires
A Rake's Guide to Seduction

What a Woman Needs

Anthologies
At the Duke's Wedding
(featuring novella *When I Met My Duchess*)
At the Christmas Wedding
(featuring novella *Map of a Lady's Heart*)
At the Billionaire's Wedding
(featuring novella *Will You Be My Wi-Fi?*)
Dressed to Kiss
(featuring novella *A Fashionable Affair*)

Short Stories
(available as e-books only)
Written in My Heart
Like None Other

Get notifed about new releases! Join my VIP readers' list at www.CarolineLinden.com/signup.html for sneak peeks, exclusive bonus content, and a free short story, *The Truth About Love*, only for members.

Caroline Linden

Will You Be My Wi-Fi?

Originally published in

At the Billionaire's Wedding

ISBN-13: 978-0-9971494-5-6

ISBN-10: 0-9971494-5-0

www.CarolineLinden.com

Printed in the USA

*For Judy, a most excellent mother-in-law.
Thank you for sharing your best recipes, and
also for raising a wonderful son.*

CHAPTER ONE

Duke Austen and Jane Sparks request the honor of your company at their wedding on August 26th. Please join the happy couple for a week of festivities and celebration . . .

Archer Quinn turned over the expensive invitation. It was a quarter-inch thick and gold-edged, but it didn't list a location. "That's weird," he muttered.

His secretary Denise looked up. "Something wrong, Mr. Quinn?"

"One of my clients is getting married." He looked around for the envelope. "But I have no idea where." He tapped open the envelope and let the enclosed cards fall into his hand. One was the RSVP card with the dates of the event, which noted in small type that the wedding was being held in England, but precise directions would be disclosed only upon receipt of a guest's acceptance, for privacy reasons. "I knew he was getting married, but I didn't expect to be invited."

"Who is it?"

"Duke Austen."

Her eyebrows went up. "That will be quite an event. Are you going?"

Archer smiled halfheartedly. A week of festivities, the invitation said; he couldn't fathom taking off that much time just to attend a wedding, not even a client's wedding.

On the other hand, Duke Austen was no ordinary client. His company, Project-TK Industries, had gone public last year to the tune of nearly twenty billion. Austen was the It Guy of Silicon Valley at the moment, riding high on a wave of genius, ballsiness, and tabloid fascination. Archer had met him in a hotel bar a few months ago and spent the evening reminiscing about epic gaming sessions battling the Covenant as Master Chief in *Halo*, only to get a call two days later asking him to represent Project-TK.

It was a lawyer's wet dream come true, particularly a freshly minted partner looking to make a splash at his new firm. Archer had talked through the engagement terms with Project-TK's company counsel, hung up the phone, and almost punched a hole in his office wall from elation. And when he told Jack Harper, the managing partner, Jack took him out for a drink. "I knew we made the right call hiring you away from San Francisco," his new boss had declared, beaming over his third glass of scotch. "Damned right!"

Still, a week in England didn't fit his current workload. "I don't think I can," he said, answering Denise's question. "Too much going on here." He was up to his eyeballs in work on a start-up called Brightball which, if all went well, would follow in Project-TK's very profitable footsteps. If all went badly because Archer vanished for a week . . . he'd have plenty of time for vacation when Jack kicked his ass out.

"Of course. Still . . ." Denise hesitated, then leaned forward. "It will be very romantic, I'm sure. He fell in love with a novelist and she wrote her books inspired by their love affair."

Archer gave her a wary, sideways glance. "What?" Romantic love affairs were not what came to mind when he thought about Austen. Obviously the man must have some moves, if he was getting married, but he was also rich, and in Archer's experience money made a lot of women blind to personality defects.

"Didn't you know?" Denise suddenly looked like an eager teenager who'd just discovered her favorite band was coming to town. "It was in all the papers. And the bride's novels are just lovely. Now you're invited to her wedding." There was definitely some envy in her voice.

"Right." Thank God; Denise's phone rang, and Archer escaped into his office.

He forgot all about Austen's wedding until the next morning, when he sat down at his desk and beheld a brightly colored paperback in the middle of his blotter. *The Wicked Wallflower,* it read in curling letters, above the image of a woman in a long gown tearing the shirt off a man who lived at the gym, judging from his muscle definition. It took Archer a moment to puzzle out why such a book was on his desk. He took it to the secretarial bay.

"Um, Denise?" he began, leaning over the side of her station and holding it up in question.

She blushed, which was very atypical for her. Denise was usually unflappable. "Yes, it's mine. I know you haven't quite decided to go yet, but I thought just in case——"

"That's very"—*What?* he wondered. *Unexpected? Strange? Somewhat disturbing?*—"thoughtful, but I don't have much time to read . . ."

Her blush grew redder. Even the tips of her ears were pink. "Oh, well—I think it's a marvelous story and I bet you would enjoy it if you read it, but really I was hoping . . . if you did decide to go to the wedding . . . that you might ask her to sign it. The bride is the author and I would love to have it autographed."

Archer cleared his throat, hoping he wasn't blushing too. "Right. I just—right. Sorry." Now he was stuck. He imagined himself approaching the bride—a woman he had never met—and asking her to sign this book. Not for him, but for his secretary. Yeah, everyone would believe that. He caught another glimpse of the cover guy's sculpted abs, and resolved to work out more often. "If I go, I will definitely have her sign it for you."

The smile on her face made him feel guilty that he'd all but decided to decline. "That would be simply wonderful, Mr. Quinn."

"Call me Archer," he reminded her and went back to work.

But he still hadn't sent the RSVP two days later when his phone rang and Duke Austen himself was on the other end. After twenty minutes of rapid-fire questions about business, Austen suddenly asked, "Did you get the wedding invitation?"

"Yep." Archer reached for his bag and rummaged inside for the thick envelope. "Congratulations to you both. Where is it?"

"England. Jane wanted to have it in a real Regency mansion," said Austen, without a lick of concern for any inconvenience it might cause his guests to have the wedding three thousand miles from home. "We had to make a last-minute change after there was a fire at the original venue. We're keeping it low-key because I want privacy. We've got this whole place for the week—sorry, Jane calls it a sennight—so come whenever you want."

"Ah," began Archer, caught off guard. "I was checking my calendar—"

"It's not for a few weeks," said Duke as if that solved every problem. "Call my assistant and she'll book everything for you. I know you're a busy guy and Jane's got a whole system set up."

"Right," said Archer, digging out the RSVP card and trying to phrase his very polite, appreciative, but negative reply. "I'm not sure—"

"It'll be a good time. And we can discuss some new ideas without people breathing down my neck. Going public has some serious baggage."

Archer made a noise of quiet agreement. Public company governance was probably cramping Duke's freewheeling, agile business style, but that was the cost of taking other people's money.

"So I'll see you there," said his client almost absently. In the background was the furious clicking of a keyboard, as if he was already at work on his next killer app. "Good talking to you, Archer."

"And to you," said Archer as the dial tone echoed in his ear. He hung his head and pulled off the earpiece with one hand. His other hand still held the pen, poised over the "Is unable to attend" box of the RSVP card. The wedding was in less than a month, and now Duke expected him to be there. He went looking for Jack Harper.

"Of course you should go," was Jack's

pronouncement.

"For a week? Brightball is getting desperate for funding." A start-up like Brightball needed venture capital to grow; they needed lawyers to make sure they didn't give away the store in exchange for that capital.

Jack waved it away. "And Project-TK will be a few million dollars in billing this year alone. You could find three more Brightballs at the wedding reception."

"So you're okay with it?"

"Go," exclaimed Jack. "I can handle Brightball; it's my client, after all. Go schmooze the hell out of Austen's friends."

And that was that. On the way back to his office, Archer walked by Denise's station. "I'm going to get your book signed for you," he told her.

She brightened. "Oh, thank you! And just think— you'll get to see the wedding of the year."

"Can't wait," he replied as he went back to work, and tried not to think about the wedding of the year.

Three weeks and two days later, Archer remembered all his hesitations and then some. Too busy to leave? Check; he spent all six hours of the overnight flight working. Too remote an acquaintance to justify being there? Check; Denise had followed reports about the wedding in the major tabloids, and breathlessly related all the juicy gossip. People Archer had never heard of—and worse, people he *had* heard of—were rumored to be on the guest list. A-list movie stars, top tech gurus, big names in finance and politics, even a few minor royals . . . He was sorry he'd agreed to go even before he had to pack. And that was all before he got off the train in the tiny town of Melbury, England, where a hired car was waiting to take him to the hotel . . . which appeared to be in the middle of Sherwood Forest.

"Are we almost there?" he asked, not so much because he was anxious to arrive but because he was starting to hope the driver had made a mistake or a wrong turn. All he could see now were trees and hedges. Did utilities even run this far into the wilderness? Duke Austen had said he wanted privacy, but this was ridiculous.

"Yes, nearly," shouted the man back, grinding his gears as the car lurched to one side. The narrow road was one sharp, blind turn after another and Archer had long since taken hold of the strap above the door. "Just another mile."

Holy crap. Another mile of this. He leaned down to peer out the window. More trees. More hedges. Very rustic—and utterly unlike any place he would have guessed likely to host the wedding of a brand new tech billionaire. Why didn't the bride want a Caribbean wedding on the beach? Why couldn't her wedding planner have talked her into a private cruise in the Mediterranean, or a week in Fiji? If money was no object, why would any bride choose to have her big day in a place that made the moon look accessible?

Denise had told him all about the bride's novels, most of which he didn't remember. But he had retained two bits of information, both of which were assuming the aspect of bad omens: the bride wrote historical romance novels, set in stately old mansions, and she was rumored to be planning a wedding that would have made Jane Austen die of envy. He devoutly hoped this wasn't going to be a nineteenth-century wedding in more ways than one.

After another several minutes of being thrown from side to side along what passed for a road, the driver pointed. "There, you see it? Brampton House."

Archer exhaled quietly. It was indeed a sprawling mansion, right out of a PBS Masterpiece movie. The grounds looked nice, and one could only see a few construction vehicles off to the side. But his suspicious eyes noted the absence of utility wires, and when he dared a quick look at his phone, it showed a grimmer sight: zero bars of cellular service.

The driver pulled right up to the impressive flight of stone steps and leapt out to unload the luggage. Archer pressed a nice tip into his hand and took one of the man's cards. Who knew when he might need an escape vehicle?

The wide oak doors at the top of the stairs stood open. As the driver set the last of his luggage on the graveled drive, a man in an expensive suit came out to meet him. He had the broad cheekbones and impeccable grooming of a male model. "Welcome to Brampton House. I am Mark Delancey, the manager."

"Nice to meet you." Archer put out his hand automatically. "Archer Quinn."

The fellow shook his hand. "May I show you to your room? Mr. Harry Compton, who owns Brampton House, extends you a warm welcome on behalf of Mr. Austen and Miss Sparks." Behind his back two younger men, also clad in well-tailored suits, were collecting the luggage and carrying it inside. Unconsciously Archer straightened his shoulders and wondered if he'd be the scruffiest man at this wedding, even including the hotel staff.

He took the opportunity to scope out the house as he followed Mr. Delancey inside. Just as fancy on the inside as it was on the outside, with sleek marble floors and intricately carved woodwork around every doorway. The ceiling above put him in mind of a room in Buckingham Palace, which he'd seen on a tour a few years back. The stairs were wide and graceful, with a rich red runner up the middle and an ornate brass railing. They climbed two flights, then turned down a long corridor with doors on one side and tall narrow windows on the other.

"The property is still undergoing a bit of renovation," said the manager as he unlocked—with a real key, not a card key—a door almost at the corner. "A few rooms aren't quite ready, and Mr. Compton suggests you avoid them for your convenience. The library is the main one still in disarray, but if you find a door barred here or there, please don't be alarmed. The builders will do their utmost to keep noise and dust to a minimum so you can enjoy your stay with us."

"I'm sure it will be fine." Archer went into the room at the manager's silent invitation, and slung his laptop bag onto the desk chair. The room wasn't a typical hotel room, but only for the better. The windows were the same tall, narrow ones as in the corridor, and the room was flooded with light. The desk was wide and the bed looked comfortable. He walked to the window and looked out on rolling hills, stately oaks, and part of a garden. It was beautiful and peaceful and screamed of money. Even way out in the country, this much land—and a house this old and tastefully renovated—must cost a fortune.

The porters brought in his luggage and arranged it neatly and quickly on luggage stands, then left. Archer turned around to find the manager still waiting by the door. "Have many other wedding guests arrived?"

"Only a few, Mr. Quinn, but that will soon change.

Mr. Austen has reserved the entire house for the wedding party, and we're expecting every room to be taken." He smiled again. The man looked like he could be on a magazine cover, or maybe on one of the bride's novel covers. "If you require anything at all, simply ask."

"I will. Thanks very much."

Mr. Delancey bowed his head and left. Archer exhaled and pulled out his phone, hoping its mute state was pure coincidence. Normally it buzzed with incoming messages or e-mail every minute or two, and it had been suspiciously silent since he left the train station. It was midafternoon now, which meant morning back at the firm's offices in Boston. He began every day with dozens of messages and e-mails, and only got more every hour, so he wasn't much surprised to see that the phone still had no signal. He dropped it on the bed and unpacked his bags, shaking his head as he hung his suits in the old-fashioned wardrobe in place of a closet.

The computer bag sat like an unexploded bomb on the desk. Archer considered ignoring it and stretching his legs with a walk through the garden, then reluctantly unzipped the bag and took out his laptop. Just a quick skim through messages, he told himself. As long as nothing was going horribly wrong with any clients, he would be justified in taking a day off. He'd left one of the firm's best associates, Elle Williams, in charge of most of his current matters while he was gone, but he still felt the need to check over her shoulder.

He found the Internet cable and the handsomely printed card with instructions for connecting, but when he plugged in, nothing came up. The indicator just blinked. He double-checked all the connections, undid them and reconnected, and still got nothing.

"Perfect place for an Internet billionaire's wedding," he said under his breath before snatching the key and heading off to find the manager.

He went back down the stairs and located the main desk, tastefully and discreetly tucked at the back of the wide airy hall. "I can't seem to get the Internet working in my room," he told the same suave gentleman who had shown him in.

"Ah yes." Mr. Delancey assumed a face one might wear at a state funeral. "I'm afraid we're having a technical problem with the cabling, sir."

Archer's bad feeling returned, worse than ever. "Have you tried rebooting the modem?"

"British Telecom will be arriving within a few days to repair it. I assure you we're working as hard as we can to restore service."

"Restore? You mean there's *no Internet?*" He'd been right: it was going to be a nineteenth-century wedding all the way.

"I'm afraid not, at the moment."

Archer just stood there. The concept of no Internet access left him speechless. Not at the moment? For how long, then—hours? Days? The whole week?

The manager was still talking. "I do apologize. Mr. Compton deeply regrets the inconvenience. If you require connectivity urgently, several shops and restaurants in town offer wireless, and of course one can purchase a mobile access plan—"

"I'd do that, but there seems to be a distinct lack of cell signal here."

The man's polished calm didn't waver in the face of Archer's dry tone. "Yes, unfortunately the house isn't in line with the nearest towers. We're down in a valley and I'm afraid there's not much I can do. However, there are spots on the grounds with better reception. If you don't mind a bit of a walk, the top of the hill directly behind the garden offers excellent reception. I've gone up there myself to test it."

Archer sighed. "The top of the hill?" It was one thing to contemplate taking a walk to see some of the famous English landscape, and another to face a hike up a hill in order to check his e-mail. He began to feel the sleepless flight and jet lag weighing on him.

"Yes, sir, it is a lovely walk." Mr. Delancey walked out from behind the counter and toward the back of the hall. Another pair of wide wooden doors stood open there, framing a postcard-perfect vista of green hills and graveled paths into a lush garden. "Follow the path to the left—I find it offers the best reception, and there is a very handsome and comfortable gazebo if you care to sit and take in the view."

Archer summoned a grim smile. "Thanks."

Phone in hand, he headed out. Wedding of the year. Yeah, right.

CHAPTER TWO

Natalie Corcoran stood in the open doorway of her borrowed cottage and watched yet another convoy of trucks roar and choke their way up the hill. That made eight today; yesterday it had been ten, one or two at a time, all straining and grinding their gears as they went up the road that led past the house. She caught a loud exclamation that could only be a curse word in some foreign language as the low-hanging branches scraped the top of one van. Saying a few bad words of her own, she snapped a photo of the traffic with her phone and texted it to her friend Pippa with the caption *Eighth one today!* She went inside and closed the door, not that it blocked the noise, and made a mental tally of all the lies her former college roommate and erstwhile friend had told her two months ago about this house.

First lie: that the cottage was quiet and isolated.

"It's in this little town in the country called Melbury," Pippa had said. "Actually not even in the town, it's at least a mile or two from it. You'll love it. Amaryllis goes there when she's on a creative binge and doesn't want to speak to anyone for weeks at a time." Amaryllis was Pippa's stepmother, moderately famous for her blown glass artwork and infamous in the British tabloids for her affairs with young footballers. Currently Amaryllis was in Albufeira, according to Pippa, soaking up sun and searching for inspiration.

"But I'm going to need access to a high quality market," Natalie had reminded her. "I'm writing a cookbook." Supposed to be, at any rate. Privately, she wasn't sure anyone would want a cookbook by her, but she had needed a face-saving reason for her sudden and abrupt absence from her family's restaurant. She could hardly tell her parents that she might kill her brother, or he might kill her, if she stayed; writing a cookbook had seemed like a brilliant excuse. Her mother, a chef, was delighted. Her father, a restaurateur recovering from a stroke, approved. And her brother Paul would just be happy she was out of his way so he could continue trying to ruin everything that made her parents' pride and joy special—or, as he called it, expanding their brand.

"There's a local market right in town," Pippa promised. "Just walk down and get as many organic eggs and as much fresh bacon as you need."

"Will it be filled with tourists?" Not that she had anything against tourists, but she was feeling a little anti-social and wanted peace. "Are there going to be people snapping pictures of the house from the road?"

Phillipa snorted. "No one ever finds that cottage. Melbury is perfectly ordinary, and it's not close to anything especially historical or scenic. Honestly, I thought I would die of boredom when I crashed with Amaryllis for a few weeks. It's the house that time forgot."

"Whoa. I need a real kitchen, Pip." Natalie had wondered if Pippa even knew what a real kitchen looked like. She'd certainly never needed to know; Pippa's father had made a fortune in banking before driving his Ferrari into a brick wall. In college, Pippa was infamous for almost burning down their apartment building by microwaving soup that was still in the can. Natalie would have bet good money she had never cooked anything in her life.

"Of course it's got a kitchen. Amaryllis thinks she can cook, so she put in everything state-of-the-art." There was a pause. "I'm sure it all works."

In fairness, Natalie had to admit Pippa had been right about the kitchen. Everything was absolutely up to date—although she was still puzzling out the idiosyncrasies of the massive AGA cooker—and it all worked splendidly. The icing on the cake was the walk-in wine cooler, which was mostly empty of wine at the moment and therefore a perfect giant refrigerator. Judged solely on the merits of the kitchen, Primrose Cottage was ideal.

But the second lie: no one would bother her.

"It's honestly in the middle of nowhere," Pippa had assured her. "There aren't even neighbors. The only house within two miles is an old manor house, and I think it's been condemned. No one lives there, the owners have moved to Bali. You can cook eighteen hours a day and never see a soul unless you go into town."

That had tipped her over the brink. Natalie was not by nature a remote or shy person, but the last year had left some serious scars on her psyche. A year ago, everything had been great. Her parents had still been in charge of the family restaurant, Cuisine du Jude, her mother in the kitchen and her father in the front of the house. Natalie loved Cuisine du Jude, or just the Jude, as they called it. She'd grown up there, folding napkins when she was a kid, manning the soda fountain and busing tables when she was a teenager, then helping out in the kitchen during college under her mother's expert instruction.

Judith Corcoran had been born to cook. There was no other explanation for her deft touch with flavors and textures, her eye for a beautifully arranged plate, her attention to the smallest influence on her diner's happiness. Tom, Natalie's dad, said he was the only struggling student who gained weight while putting himself through college on a shoestring budget, because his wife could make a four-star dinner out of a buck and a half's worth of ingredients. A few years after he finished his degree in business, he'd borrowed money from every family member with a hundred dollars to spare and opened a tiny, hole-in-the-wall restaurant. Judy cooked, Tom bused and managed. Soon they moved to a bigger spot, then to a nicer one with a patio on the river, and there they'd stayed, successful but more a local gem than anything, until three years ago when a renowned restaurant critic, in town for her son's college graduation, ate at the Jude. A month later her raving review appeared in the *New York Times,* calling the Jude "the most perfect date night restaurant in the world." The national morning TV shows called. Oprah visited. Judy Corcoran was invited on cooking shows left and right. And every table in the restaurant was booked up for eight months in advance.

Then it all went to pieces.

Tom had a stroke—thankfully not a debilitating one, but bad enough to shake everything up. The doctors decreed he should not work for at least six months; Judy declared she was taking a sabbatical to care for him and oversee his rehab. Natalie, who had been cooking alongside her mother since she was six, would take over the kitchen, and Paul, who had followed their father into the business side, would run the front of the house. That was fine with

16

Natalie. The Jude had been her life, and she wanted to stay there forever, keeping up her parents' tradition.

If only Paul hadn't gotten stars in his eyes from all the national press fawning over the Jude. All on his own, he decided that one location was not enough; they needed two or three or eight. And he'd gone and hired an architect to start planning these new locations.

The fight, when Natalie found out, was epic. Worse than when they were kids. Only this one hadn't ended with a spanking or being grounded. Their mother had intervened, white-faced and furious. "Stop it," she told them both. "You are too old for this. You owe your father better. Paul, there will be no expansion without your father's approval, and he's too weak to give it. If you ask him about it, I will disinherit you now," she said as he'd opened his mouth to argue. "Natalie, things cannot stay the same forever and ever." She'd looked between the two of them in the deeply disappointed way only a mother could manage. "You're not to speak to each other for two weeks. Cool down and act like rational adults."

"What about the Jude?" Natalie had protested. "We can't run the restaurant without speaking."

"Mick can mediate," said her mother, naming the Jude's sous chef.

Natalie tried, but within a week realized it wouldn't work. It turned out she and her brother were totally capable of communicating without speaking a word, and most of their exchanged glances could be translated as *you are such an idiot*. The day Paul had the nerve to have his architect out to the restaurant for lunch, Natalie lost it and dumped a bowl of soup on her brother. Paul called her crazy. Natalie called him a lying snake. Mick called their mother.

Writing a cookbook had been the only straw

Natalie could grasp to save face. Banished from the Jude, she had to get away, as far away as possible, from her brother's subtle gloating. He wasn't getting his way just yet, but she'd blown her cred as the sane, sensible child and they both knew it. Thank God for Pippa, who had volunteered this cottage—a cooking paradise far enough removed from Massachusetts that she wouldn't be able to embarrass herself again. Even if Pippa had warned her it was next to a construction zone, she would have gone, but she'd gotten used to the relative quiet. The last week or so had made her feel like she was living in the middle of a highway.

Her phone buzzed. "Bloody hell," cried Pippa. Dance music throbbed behind her voice. "What the hell is going on?"

"Beats me, but it's big." She checked the clock. "Are you at a club at three in the afternoon?"

"But no one lives there! We used to traipse over the hill to have smokes when we were kids because it was deserted." A high-pitched laugh shrilled in the background. "Hang on, let me see if Amaryllis knows." The line went dead.

Natalie stayed where she was. After extensive trial and error and a great deal of cursing, she had mapped the irregular spots of cell coverage on the property. This spot right inside the kitchen door offered up to three bars, which was excellent by local standards. Near the window in the front bedroom upstairs one could usually get two bars, and the back bath sometimes got two. Pippa had warned her that she'd have to walk up the hill to get a steady three bars, or even four if the gods were feeling kind, but that was too much trouble. Natalie just left her phone in one of the more likely locations with the ringer turned up. Not that she wanted people to call her, as she was supposed to be a hermit these two months, but her mother would freak out if she didn't answer.

A few minutes later the phone went off again. "Oh my God. I swear I had no idea—Amaryllis says the Melburys decided to renovate the house and turn it into a hotel or some such." Pippa sounded mournful. "I am so sorry."

"Is it open?"

"I have no idea! Amaryllis said they have a website now. Hang on a mo."

Something butted Natalie's elbow. Oliver, the resident cat, pushed his round head under her arm, demanding a good pet. She scratched his ears, careful not to step out of the tiny bubble of cell reception.

"Sorry," said Pippa breathlessly. The noise behind her waned a bit. "Just ran into the coatroom. The house is called Brampton House. Google it, maybe you can find out what's going on. Although honestly, the last time I saw that house it looked like the roof would fall in, so I can't imagine how much work it needs."

That would explain the many vans and trucks struggling up the road. Natalie let her head fall back and stuck out her tongue at the ceiling. Just her luck. Oliver meowed again and jumped down. He padded to the door and began circling expectantly, so she went to let him out. She wasn't entirely sure Oliver belonged to Primrose Cottage, but there was a bag of cat food in the pantry. Because Paul was allergic, the Corcorans had never had a pet growing up, and Natalie found she rather liked it. Oliver was the perfect male: soft and furry, easy to feed, and he purred like a vibrator when someone scratched under his chin.

"So much for peace and quiet," she said to Pippa. "Well. The hotel is a good mile away or more. If it needs that much work, it can't be open yet, so I only have to suffer the traffic . . ." She threw open the door and Oliver bounded out, only to draw up short and hiss. Natalie stared in furious disbelief. "You've got to be kidding me."

"What?" Pippa demanded. "What did you say?"

"Just tell me where the garden hose is," Natalie replied grimly. "There are two people—probably guests at the so-called hotel—having sex on your stepmother's patio."

CHAPTER THREE

It was a fifteen-minute walk to the gazebo, which did command a magnificent view as Mr. Delancey had promised. Unfortunately, the manager must have sent every other guest up the hill as well; three other people were already there when Archer reached it. A tall young man in a yellow hoodie was pacing in circles around the gazebo, talking computer code into his phone. A dark-haired girl was sprawled on one of the cushioned benches in the gazebo with her phone pressed to one ear, while an older woman was giving orders for dress alterations between hungry draws on a cigarette.

Archer walked upwind and pulled out his phone. To his relief it found signal and began downloading e-mail, though at a snail's pace. The programmer circled him— "You're killing the CPU by doing it that way . . ."—and the older woman lit a new cigarette—"I don't want it down to my ruddy ankles, I'm not some crusty old dowager!"— while the girl began filing her nails—"I can't believe we have this whole place for a week! It's, like, really old and shit . . ."

He hit two-dozen messages and walked a few steps

away, trying not to overhear. Ten more messages, when there were probably two hundred waiting to download. He scrolled through, deleting most of the e-mail as banal or unimportant, but they were all from the previous night. One by one, ten more appeared on the screen. The programmer came around again, this time agitated and waving one hand—"I don't want it to call the server that often, it will crash the whole app!"—the older woman had moved on from the length of her dress to worse—"I want some beading. What do you think? Would beading around the neckline make me look jowly?"—and the younger woman fished out a beer from a cooler beneath her bench—"Check it out! I think I can see Windsor Castle from here! Do you want me to send you a picture?"

Archer eyed the signal indicator. Three bars, flickering up to four from time to time. He drifted a little farther down the far side of the hill. If Brampton House was in a valley, shielded from cell service by that hill, then there ought to be cell service many places on the other side of the hill, not just at the top. The signal held and he walked on, watching the messages slowly accumulate. The ground flattened out into a broad gentle slope of lawn. He was almost at the bottom of the hill, but he could still hear the older woman going on about her dress: "It has to match the shoes! Don't do the damn beading if it won't match the shoes!" He kept walking.

There was a line of trees, with a thin trail leading through and beyond it. Still scrolling through messages, Archer absently followed it. A muffled noise caught his attention, and then another. He looked up, and did a double take. Just behind the trees, a guy was lying on his back in the grass, with a girl grinding on top of him. She was clothed—barely—but her skirt hid any proof of actual intercourse. Whatever was going on under her skirt, both of them were obviously enjoying themselves a great deal. Archer averted his eyes and went the other way.

It was blessedly quiet out here and the air was crisp and fresh. For the first time he started to see why Jane Sparks had liked the place enough to drag her friends and family across an ocean. It was remote, sure, but that also meant privacy. Just last week Duke and Jane had struck a deal with a major magazine for exclusive wedding photos in exchange for a generous donation to Jane's favorite charity, and having it in the middle of nowhere would make it harder for the paparazzi to find them. Archer made a mental note to keep an eye out for anyone suspicious; it would certainly be easy for someone to sneak through the woods and angle a telephoto lens on Brampton House.

And then, out of nowhere, an alert popped onto his screen, asking if he wanted to join a Wi-Fi network. Archer stopped in his tracks. He tapped an app on his phone, and realized the Wi-Fi signal was nice and strong. It was also, unfortunately, password protected.

He deliberated. It was probably unneighborly to steal someone's Wi-Fi, but he had no idea where the neighbor actually was. It wasn't even his neighbor. He tried a few common passwords, none of which worked. Well, if he couldn't stealthily join the network, maybe he could talk his way in.

The track curved and wound through a meadow, where the grass was taller. A tall hedge ran along the side, and he realized it screened the road to Brampton House. So this was what lay on the other side of all those trees. Now that he wasn't risking life and limb along the twisting road, Archer could acknowledge that it was picturesque. Still very remote and primitive for a techie wedding, but beautiful.

Around a bend in the path he found the source of the Wi-Fi signal. A house of gray stone sat in the middle of a garden, with a small patio facing him. And—he actually stopped walking and took a deep breath—the most heavenly smell drifted from the open windows.

Led by his nose, he walked right up to the edge of the patio. It smelled of chocolate and coffee, and made him realize he hadn't eaten lunch, nor anything else today other than a wholly inadequate roll from an airport kiosk, washed down with a bottle of warm water. Oh God, what he wouldn't give for a good cup of coffee right now, and if it came with a slice of chocolate cake—

The door opened with a bang, and a woman stalked out toward him. A very attractive woman, with light brown curls bouncing around her head and a mesmerizing sway to her hips. Archer started to smile, but it fell off his face as she drew near. "Whoa!"

"This is private property," she said acidly in an unmistakably American accent.

"I'm sorry, I didn't know." He took a step backward and kept his eyes on the large meat cleaver she was pointing at him. "There's no sign marking the boundary of the hotel grounds."

She seemed to bristle. "You're staying at the hotel?"

"Yes," he said warily. Her tone indicated that was not a mark in his favor.

"What the hell is going on up there?" She waved her free hand at the road. "A dozen trucks a day go up and down that road."

"Just a wedding." He kept his voice calm and unthreatening. She was holding the cleaver like she knew how to use it.

"A wedding. It's not even supposed to be open!" She shook her head, and curls spilled over her face. She swiped them back, and shaded her eyes to peer up the hill. Unthinkingly Archer gave her another quick once-over. A long white apron hid most of her, but her fitted shirt showed off a nice pair of breasts. On her feet she wore clogs, but her legs to the knee were bare. Cleaver aside, she was damn fine.

"Could you please tell everyone else at the hotel that this house, and this garden, are not part of the hotel grounds? If I find one more jackass out here—"

"I don't recommend you cleaver them, even if they trespass," he said when she pursed her lips in disgruntlement.

"What?" She stared up at him. He'd thought her eyes were brown, but now he saw they were more hazel, with gold and green sparks and only brown around the edges.

"The . . ." He motioned with one hand, still upraised in the universal gesture of surrender. "The meat cleaver. I don't think English law would pardon the use of a cleaver even on a very rude trespasser."

"Oh." She looked at it, and her face eased. All the hard lines of fury disappeared, and the look she gave him was almost sheepish. "Sorry about that. I was chopping up a chicken for pot pie when I saw you."

"And here I thought I smelled chocolate and coffee," he said. "It must be the English countryside."

She laughed—just for a moment, but enough to make his breath catch. When she smiled, she was gorgeous. "No, it's coffee and chocolate now. Chicken later, if Oliver doesn't eat it." Her eyes grew round. "Oh my God, if that cat eats my chicken—"

"That cat?" By a lucky stroke, he'd caught sight of a big gray cat napping in the sun at the edge of the patio. When the woman whirled around to see where he pointed, then exhaled in relief, Archer felt an irrational burst of relief himself. Oliver was a cat, not a guy. He wanted her to stay and keep talking to him. Preferably without the cleaver raised in his direction.

"Yes, *that* cat. He likes to help himself..." Her voice tapered off and she stood a little straighter. The smile disappeared from her face. "I'm sorry it looked like I was going to chop off your head. People from the hotel have been wandering down here and making themselves at home."

"There's no cell service there. The manager is telling everyone to go to the top of the hill, and it's gotten a bit crowded. I was just in search of peace and quiet." He showed her his phone as if it would prove his innocent intentions.

Her lips quirked. "And the couple having sex on the lounger awhile ago? I didn't see any phones, but maybe they'd left them in their clothes."

"You're kidding." She gave him a dour look, and he choked back a laugh. Apparently the horny couple had retreated to the woods only after being chased off the patio. "Okay, I have no reply to that. But I swear I was just trying to check my e-mail." He decided to take a gamble. "In fact, I noticed you're broadcasting a nice, strong Wi-Fi signal. Is there any chance you'd be willing to let me borrow your network . . . ?"

"No." She turned and headed back toward the house.

Archer scrambled after her, shoving his phone into his pocket. "The entire hotel has no Internet service;

technical issues with the cables or something. I brought a lot of work with me that I just have to get done. There's a woman on top of the hill right now, shouting into her phone about beads on her dress, and whether they'll make her look jowly or not."

"Too bad," she said without turning her head. "Not my problem."

"Of course not, but I'm not asking to impose on you. I can work out of sight. I'll pay your Internet bill for the month," he added in desperation.

She had reached the door of the house. This close to the windows, the scent of coffee and chocolate was intoxicating, and overwhelming. He felt like a junkie, shaking and salivating at the prospect of a fix. And his phone was still laboring to download messages at the slow, slow speed of British rural data networks. But the woman stopped on the step, barring the door, and crossed her arms in an unmistakable refusal. "No. I don't know you, I don't know who you are, but the answer is no. First it's just you, then half the hotel guests will be here. I do not need anyone hanging out around the patio, for Wi-Fi or afternoon sex or anything else."

"Uh." He blinked, distracted by the way she said "afternoon sex" with a tart lilt that made him wonder how opposed she really was to the idea. He was lightheaded from hunger and the tantalizing smell of chocolate, but mentioning afternoon sex was really unfair on her part. Now he had to think about it. And the way she folded her arms plumped up her breasts even more. "Right. But I swear to God I won't tell a soul where I'm getting Internet access. I don't know ninety-nine percent of them anyway."

Her brows went up in disbelief. "Really? Then why are you here?" She went inside and closed the door.

Archer jumped to the open window. "For work," he called in.

"Go away," she called back.

"Please?" he tried once more.

She gave him a glare, and slammed the cleaver down through a piece of chicken. "No!"

Archer put up his hands again and backed off. "Got it. Sorry to bother you. Good luck with the chicken."

But the smell of chocolate, and the image of her well-shaped ass striding away from him, stayed in his mind during the long walk back to Brampton House.

CHAPTER FOUR

Natalie was tinkering with the controls on the large AGA stove when there was a knock on the cottage's front door.

She considered not answering it. It was probably another wedding guest, out roaming the countryside. She shook her head, remembering the tall, good-looking American guy who'd invaded the garden yesterday—in search of Wi-Fi, of all things. Amaryllis must have the most happening patio in England, what with random people having sex on the lounger and hot guys wanting to check their e-mail there. For a moment the thought crossed her mind that if anyone had to get naked on the patio, she really would have preferred it to be the Wi-Fi guy.

She wrinkled her nose, reminding herself that she didn't really want to see anyone naked on the patio. She didn't want to see anyone, unless it was someone who could explain the quirks of the oven. She'd thought she had it solved, until she burned two trays of chocolate cookies yesterday. But when the knock sounded again at the door, she dropped the manual and went to see who it was.

A large bunch of flowers greeted her when she

opened the door. "Hello again," said the hot guy from yesterday.

"Hi." She leaned against the doorframe and resisted the urge to smile back at him. He had a really attractive dimple in one cheek when he grinned.

He made a show of looking at her hands. "Not armed today?"

"Not at the moment."

"That's a relief. I brought peace offerings." He handed her the flowers and a bag she recognized from the lone gourmet food boutique in town. "For disturbing your peace yesterday."

Intrigued, Natalie took the bag. Her brows went up as she peeked inside and saw a variety of expensive ingredients. "Tahitian vanilla and Belgian chocolate?"

"I could smell that chocolate thing you were baking yesterday in my dreams." He half-closed his eyes and an expression of rapture drifted over his face. "I think I'd kill for a plate of it."

"Here I thought you wanted my Wi-Fi password," she said lightly.

"Oh, I'd like that as well." He paused. "Do I have to choose only one?"

She folded her arms and shrugged. "You haven't got either right now."

He grinned, showing off the dimple again. "I sure don't. Archer Quinn, overworked lawyer, ignorant trespasser, and helpless chocolate lover." He put out his hand.

With only a slight hesitation she put her hand in his. "Natalie."

His grin deepened. "Very nice to meet you, Natalie."

"Likewise." At least, she thought so. He did look like a nice guy—or rather, he looked like a pretty hot guy who was acting very disarming and charming. She wondered what he really was.

"Obviously I began badly yesterday, and I came first to apologize." He cleared his throat. "It was not my intent to trespass on your property and I unreservedly apologize for any alarm it may have caused you. Furthermore, I should have introduced myself and laid to rest any fears you might have had that I was an axe murderer prowling the neighborhood."

"That's why I took my cleaver," she pointed out.

"I did notice," he agreed with a hint of a smile. "Would you have used it, if I had been an axe murderer?"

"Of course," she said in the same serious tone. "I can disembowel a whole turkey in four minutes. I doubt a man takes much longer, once you whack off the head."

He blinked. "You disemboweled a turkey? Good Lord, what did he do to you?"

Natalie snorted with laughter before she could stop herself. "Nothing. I just wanted to eat him."

He blinked again, and then his eyes warmed. "Really."

She ignored the speculative tone. "Yep. Stuffed his guts with cornbread, sage, and sausage, roasted him for three hours, and served him up on a platter. He was delicious."

Archer Quinn inhaled a ragged breath. "You've got to stop talking about food that way. Between the memory of the chocolate yesterday and the idea of a roasted turkey, I almost passed out here on your steps."

"Haven't they got good food up the hotel? I've seen enough catering vans headed up there to feed an army."

"It's hotel food," he said, as if that explained everything. "You can't smell it baking. My mother used to make this chocolate pudding cake . . . It was my favorite thing in the world."

"Chocolate pudding cake, huh."

"With vanilla ice cream on top." He winked. "The way to this man's heart."

For some reason her cheeks felt hot. "I was asking in a purely professional capacity. I'm working on a cookbook."

"Really?" He perked up. "If you need any samples tasted, I'd be glad to help out."

Natalie shook her head. "First you want free Internet, now free food. Thank you for the flowers, Mr. Quinn, but I have to get back to work—"

"So do I," he said hastily. "But I need reliable Internet to do it."

She pursed her lips, unwillingly charmed by the flowers and Tahitian vanilla. "What do you do again?"

"I'm a lawyer." He pulled out his wallet and handed her a business card. *Archer Quinn, Partner, Harper Millman LLP*, it read, with an address in Boston.

She frowned. The lawyer Paul had hired as part of his expansion plans had been an arrogant prick, with a full head of white hair and a flashy Rolex. He'd treated her as if she were a child throwing a temper tantrum when she didn't agree with Paul's ideas. "I don't like lawyers."

"No, no, no," he said quickly as she straightened, preparing to close the door. "I'm a very harmless sort of lawyer. I just write boring business memos."

She paused, one hand on the door. "I really need peace and quiet."

"And I will not bother you," he promised. "You won't hear one peep from me."

Natalie deliberated. He had good gift sense. He appreciated the smell of baking. These two things had an outsized effect on her judgment. Also, he was very kind to the eyes, as her mother would say, and she was hardly immune to that. "You can't come in the house."

"I don't need to," he replied at once. "The signal on the patio is excellent."

She frowned again. "How do you know that?"

"Phone app." His teasing grin reappeared. "How about a trial of a few days?"

That dimple was dangerous. Natalie poked around in the gift bag to avoid meeting his brilliant gaze. Belgian chocolate, threads of saffron, imported balsamic vinegar, even a bottle of wine. She lifted it an inch to read the label and barely suppressed a start of surprise. He must have spent well over a hundred bucks on all this. "I suppose a day or two couldn't hurt."

"Great." He sounded relieved. "Thank you."

"Why do you need to work so desperately? Aren't you here for a big fancy wedding with all sorts of events?"

He laughed a little sadly. "If only. The groom is my client; he invited me because . . . I'm not quite sure. But the work can't wait, so I'll have to miss whatever wedding festivities are planned."

Natalie fiddled with the bottle of wine. "Boring business memos, huh."

"Lots of them," he said glumly.

She gave in to the pull. He would stay out on the patio, and if she snuck a peek from time to time, it wouldn't hurt anyone. It might even do her good to exchange a word with someone other than Oliver from time to time. "All right. Whenever you want, the patio is yours."

His face eased into a more honest smile. The dimple was back, and crinkles appeared around his dark blue eyes. God, he was good-looking. "How about now?"

Archer had left his laptop case out of sight. Just bringing it with him seemed to taunt fate, but thankfully Natalie was agreeably softened up by his apology gift. He'd gone all out on that, because an extensive ramble of the Brampton House grounds hadn't turned up any other source of Internet. He supposed he could go sit in one of the cafés in town, as Mr. Delancey kept suggesting, but he much preferred a quieter place to work. The patio behind her house began to look idyllic, especially after he ran into the hotel owner, Harry Compton, who confirmed—reluctantly—that the Internet at Brampton House was well and truly screwed until British Telecom deigned to come repair it. The Wi-Fi signal at the stone house became his only hope.

And blessedly his gamble had paid off. He scooted the patio table a little more into the shade of the brick wall that ran down one side of the garden, and opened his computer. It had taken over an hour for his e-mail to finish downloading yesterday. Even slow Wi-Fi would be an improvement, and there was a chance she'd bake something delicious again to perfume the air.

"Here." She came out the kitchen door with a scrap of paper in one hand. "You'll need the password."

Primrose123, he typed in, quietly elated when his laptop connected and the Wi-Fi indicator blinked to full strength. "Thanks. Why primrose?"

She stopped in a patch of sun and blinked. Her hair looked reddish gold in the sunlight. "This house is called Primrose Cottage. It used to be part of the Brampton House estate, I think, like an old-fashioned mother-in-law quarters."

He grinned. "That explains why it's separated from the main house by a hill."

She snorted with laughter. "I didn't hear that! My mom would make an excellent mother-in-law."

"So would mine," he returned, "but I understand why it's on the other side of the hill."

She shook her head and went inside, closing the door. Still grinning, Archer got to work.

He hadn't been wrong. Working on the patio was idyllic. There was a cool breeze, but plenty of sun warming the air. It was quiet, with only the rustling of the plants and an occasional noise of pots clanking or water running from inside the kitchen. The Internet wasn't blazing fast, but it was quick enough that he could remotely connect to his desktop in Boston. And then there was the smell. She was baking blueberry pie, he guessed; not as good as chocolate cake, but still mouthwatering aromas.

After a while the kitchen door opened. Deep in a dense paragraph about corporate director elections, Archer didn't look up until she stopped beside his table.

"I have a favor to ask," she said. In her hands was a tray with five small plates, each one containing a mound of blue-violet blueberries and crust, and a tall glass of water.

"Does it involve eating anything on that tray?" His stomach growled at the thought. Archer glanced at his watch and saw with a start that it was past two o'clock. And he hadn't brought lunch.

"It involves tasting everything on this tray, and giving me an honest evaluation of the samples. You did offer."

He closed his laptop and pushed it to the far end of the table without taking his eyes off the tray. "A gentleman keeps his word. Bring it on."

She set down the tray and placed one plate in front of him. A wavering number "1" was drizzled in chocolate sauce on the far edge of the plate. "Let's start with this."

Gingerly Archer scooped a bite onto the fork and tasted it. For a moment he let it sit on his tongue, then he began to chew, until his eyes drifted closed in bliss. The berries were tiny and tender and bursting with juice. "It's good," he managed to say, spearing another bite.

"In what way?" Natalie drew a small notebook from her apron pocket and made a note. "Is it too sweet? Too chewy?"

He chewed more carefully this time, thinking. "No, not too sweet. There's something else in it . . ." Another bite, this time with more biscuit-like crust. "Something sharp. Not my favorite, but still edible."

"Ginger." She wrote some more. "Next sample."

He took the plate drizzled with a "2" and dug in. "This has more than blueberries," he said in surprise.

"Blackberries," she muttered. "Good, or not?"

Archer ate some more. Each plate held only a few bites, so he tried to concentrate on each one. "Not as good as just blueberries."

He tasted his way through two more plates, washing each one down with a good drink of water. Once the initial Pavlovian reaction to the sight of food—dessert, no less—had ebbed, he found himself watching his hostess. Now her hair was tied back with a red kerchief around her head, and there was a tiny gold heart on a chain around her neck. Her apron was covered with dark blue blotches of blueberry juice, and she must have an itch on one leg; from time to time she would lift one foot and rub the toe down the back of her other ankle. It was oddly sexy.

"Last one." She set the fifth and final plate in front of him.

"Just as I was getting good at this," he joked, reaching for the fork. "At least, I hope. Am I getting good at this? Is it helpful?"

She nodded. "Definitely! I've baked all these a hundred times. It's good to have someone else's opinion to make sure I'm not just reinforcing my own inclinations."

"What kind of cookbook are you working on?"

"My family owns a restaurant. I'm writing a cookbook based on my mother's recipes from the kitchen there."

"It must be sold out every night, if this is what the food tastes like."

Her mouth twisted in a bitter way. "Something like that. What do you think of number five?"

Obediently he took a bite. What was wrong with the restaurant? God knew he wanted to eat there now, if only for the desserts. "It's got . . ." He concentrated on the plate in front of him. "It's got lemon in it."

"Very good." A faint smile crossed her face as she wrote on her notebook. "Anything else?"

"Yes." He took another bite. "This is the best one, by the way. Is it cinnamon?"

"And cloves. Why is it the best?"

Archer scraped up another bite. "I have no idea, but it's unbelievable. Would it be rude if I licked the plate?"

She laughed and put the notebook back in her

apron pocket. "Not rude, but a little gross. You just ate half a blueberry cobbler."

"And loved every bite of it." He regarded the empty plates with some sadness. "What were you testing, with these five?"

"Variations on flavorings. I have a base recipe, but wanted to add subtle changes to allow for different tastes. One has more exotic flavors like ginger and five spices, one has nutmeg and lemon, one has cinnamon and cloves . . ." She stopped and looked sheepish. "Do you cook?"

"No, but I am a very appreciative diner." He grinned, and she laughed. "My mother is an excellent cook."

"Chocolate pudding cake," she said.

"Angels in heaven don't know what they're missing in my mother's chocolate pudding cake."

Natalie smiled. "I'd love to have that recipe."

"Well, I'd like to taste your version of it. I mean that literally," he said when Natalie kept on smiling. She was gorgeous when she smiled. "I'll get the recipe, and we'll see if you can make it as well as she can."

Her smile faded a bit. "I doubt it." A chill seemed to blow across the patio. "You don't have to get it on my account."

Archer could have smacked his own forehead. What had he said? Didn't women love a man who adored his mother's cooking? Or did that make him look like a mama's boy who would forever find other women lacking? "No trouble," he said lightly. "She'll think I'm wasting away on bad takeout and overnight me a frozen cake. So even if you never bake it, I still win."

She busied herself with the dishes. "Suit yourself. Thanks again for your help."

"No prob—whoa!" The big gray cat had jumped into his lap. "Hey there, cat."

Natalie set down the tray with a clink. "Oliver! Come here!"

Archer scratched the cat's head as it began purring and kneading his shirt collar. "He's fine. Just really big."

"He's enormous," said Natalie with a sigh. "I only feed him one scoop of kitty food a day."

"I bet this garden is free of mice and voles, though."

"Ew." She looked askance at the cat. "I let him sleep on my bed."

Lucky cat, thought Archer. "He's an outdoorsman, used to hunting for his dinner." The cat certainly still had claws, which were digging into his chest now. He put Oliver down, giving him a few rough strokes down the back as the cat's purr grew louder.

"He's not mine," she said, as if that explained her revulsion at the cat's predatory tendencies. "He just belongs to the house, which is also not mine."

That was interesting. He could tell from her voice she was American, but apparently she was also just visiting. He found himself far too interested in Natalie the baker. "So where's the restaurant?" he asked, trying to get back to a happier topic that might make her smile again.

It didn't work. If anything, her expression grew harder. "In Wellesley, outside Boston."

He perked up, choosing to ignore her frosty answer. Not only was she American, she came from his new home state. "Hey, I just moved to Boston! Which direction is Wellesley from the city?"

"West." She picked up the tray. "Thanks for tasting."

"You're welcome," he said to her retreating back. She didn't look at him again, and the door closed behind her with a bang. Archer looked at Oliver, now rolling on his back in a spot of sun. "You could have warned me." He leaned down and gave the cat a quick rub on the belly. "Any other subjects I should avoid? No? Maybe? Thanks for the advice." Oliver just purred, flexing his feet in the air. Archer sighed, cast one more glance at the firmly closed kitchen door, and went back to corporate director elections.

CHAPTER FIVE

For the next two days, Archer Quinn appeared on her patio. Natalie knew he was there early, because she checked every morning when she came downstairs. He liked the mornings, she thought; he arrived before nine every day with a travel mug of coffee. True to his word he kept out of her way and never knocked on the door. He spent a fair amount of time talking on his phone. The kitchen became unbearably hot with the giant AGA on, so she had to keep the windows open, and that meant she listened to his voice in the background. Even without making out most of his words, she came to like the sound of his voice. More tenor than bass, but with a little rasp to it. After a while she could distinguish between callers. Most of them sounded like business colleagues, from the random bits of conversation she overheard, but there was someone called Elle who made him laugh. Natalie found herself wondering who it was, and in a moment of weakness she looked up the firm on his business card. Elle Williams was another lawyer there. Natalie wondered if he was dating her, or wanted to date her, then she called herself an idiot and walked away from the computer. It was none of her business.

There was one significant benefit to his presence. At least twice, other wedding guests wandered into her garden, and before she could go set them straight, Archer did it for her. Apparently there was still no Internet to be had at the hotel, and more than one guest had followed the same path to her Wi-Fi signal. Without ever giving away that he had the password, Archer pointed them in the direction of town and described the best spots for cell phone reception. Natalie wondered if he also told them the crazy woman in Primrose Cottage was liable to come after them with a meat cleaver, but if he did, she never overheard it.

She could see why he made a good lawyer, though. He was friendly without being smarmy, never rude, and had a logical argument for everything. Everyone seemed to part from him on good terms. Even his phone calls were cordial and good-humored, which didn't fit with her view of lawyers.

Not that it was any of her business.

She was whipping egg whites when her phone rang. She pushed the heavy stand mixer away from the counter edge and reached for her phone. "Oh, hi, Mom."

"Hi, sweetie. How are you?"

"Whipping up some meringue today. The weather is perfect for it."

"That's my girl," said Judy Corcoran with approval. "What are you making?"

Natalie turned back to the mixer and caught a glimpse of Archer. There was a thin frown of concentration between his brows as he typed away. The sun fell across his shoulders, making them look very broad, and shone on the top of his head, picking out the bit of wave in his sandy hair. With some effort, she pulled her eyes away.

"Natalie?"

"Um, cake," she blurted. "I've been doing desserts for over a week now. The pies are done, as are the cobblers and the ice creams. I have four kinds of cake on my list, then a few more cookies, and I'll be done with dessert."

"Sounds like a good pace." Her mother's voice softened. "And how *are* you?"

She stopped the mixer and checked the egg whites. Almost ready. She turned it back on. "Just fine, Mom. How is Dad?"

"He's doing very well. The physical therapist has him writing letters now, so he wrote a long list of instructions for Paul."

She knew her mother had done it on purpose, but the mention of her brother was a bridge too far. "That's great. I remember the little notes Dad used to put in my school lunches. I miss those notes."

"And how about your brother?"

"I don't miss him as much," she replied evenly. "Can we talk about something else?"

Her mother's sigh was sad. "When are you going to be ready to talk to Paul?"

Never. She debated ending the call and blaming it on the meringue. "Not now."

"He was wrong, Nat, but so were you," her mother admonished. "I know you just want what's best for the Jude—"

"But we can't agree on what that is, Mom. He wants to make us a franchise and open eight more locations. He wants to take on millions in debt and put our name on restaurants all the way across the country. I just don't think that's a good idea. It will ruin everything I love about the Jude."

"Not everything, I hope," said her mother tartly. "I'll still be there, as will your dad. What do *you* want to do?"

Natalie hit the switch on the mixer and stared out the window. It was a gorgeous view, one she'd become accustomed to, and one she would miss when she finally had to return to the States. It was even better with Archer sitting off to one side, now leaning back in his chair and holding his phone to his ear. "I don't know, Mom," she said softly, right at the same moment Archer said, "Hey, Elle, is this a good time?"

His voice carried across the stone patio, through the open window. "Is someone there?" asked Judy.

Natalie cringed. "Yeah. Well, no, not really. It's just someone borrowing the Internet connection."

"Someone?"

She heard the veiled curiosity in her mother's question. "There's a fancy hotel nearby, apparently, and they're hosting a big wedding. Their Internet went out and one guy walked over and persuaded me to let him use the Wi-Fi here."

"I hope he's a nice guy."

It occurred to her that here was the perfect distraction from Paul. "Seems very nice, so far."

"Really?" Judy was losing her noncommittal tone, edged out by interest. "Good-looking?"

She watched Archer stretch one arm over his head and grin at something Elle said. Colleagues, or more? *Not her business.* "Yes," she murmured absently to her mother.

"And he's in your house? Every day?"

Natalie snapped out of her momentary trance. "Not

in the house, he sits on the patio and works on his laptop. I'm working, too, remember?"

"The way to a man's heart is through his stomach," said her mother. "Take him something to eat."

"Mom! I am not trying to—to—"

"What?" asked her unrepentant mother. "You don't have to shag him—isn't that what they call it over there? It sounds so British. But it's how I got your father, and I just think—"

"Oh, Mom, my meringue is ready," Natalie exclaimed, snapping the mixer on full speed and leaning down so the whir of the motor filled the line. "Gotta go, give Dad a kiss for me, bye!" She ended the call and almost threw the phone across the counter.

Ugh. Was her mother having some kind of midlife crisis? Natalie had friends whose mothers were almost rabid about seeing them married with a few kids. Her mom had never been that way . . . although she had always been the most open parent about discussing sex, which had mortified Natalie and Paul to no end. She'd once offered to buy condoms for any of their friends, which was just too much to contemplate. Natalie admitted her mother's openness was wonderful when she actually wanted to talk about something delicate, but other times . . . ugh.

And if her mother could see Archer . . . She dared another glance at the patio. He was still on the phone, now using a headset. He moved his hands as he talked, almost like he was sculpting his words in the air. Her gaze lingered on his hands for a moment, on those long expressive fingers. Mom would approve. Mom *did* approve, without even seeing him.

"Idiot," she told herself, and went back to her meringue.

Now that he was keeping his head above water with work, Archer began to enjoy being in England. There were events for the wedding guests every day, but he mostly skipped them in favor of walking down to Primrose Cottage. It was quite pleasant working on Natalie's patio. Every day some new delicious smell would drift out her windows, although she didn't ask him to taste anything else. Archer spent a shameful amount of time trying to guess what she was making every day. He fantasized about peach cobbler, chocolate cookies, and strawberry pie—and increasingly about Natalie herself. Just the sight of her through the kitchen window stoked his interest.

Even when he didn't strictly need to work, he walked down to the cottage. There was always something he could do for some client, after all. True to his promise, Jack was handling the work for Brightball, although Archer had stepped in to answer a few questions. Bill, the founder, was excitable, and Archer could tell he was absorbed in something that had him keyed up. Hopefully it was some innovative invention. Distracted by the aromas from the kitchen, as well as the glimpses of Natalie herself, Archer didn't pay it too much mind. Brightball was Jack's client, after all.

But he did need to focus on his top client when they met. Duke Austen had been only a fleeting presence as far as Archer knew; he must be occupied with wedding preparations and rehearsals and whatever else went into planning the wedding of the year. So much for talking about new ventures or any other business. The wedding planner, a dark-haired intense woman named Arwen

Kilpatrick, seemed to be everywhere at once with a schedule in her hand, often with the hotel owner Mr. Compton at her side. Archer hoped she was giving him hell about the lack of Internet and reliable cell service.

Still, Archer thought he'd better go to the cocktail hour, even though he knew very few of the other guests. Contrary to Denise's tabloid scouting, there were no movie stars or royals at the event, but Jack Harper's prediction that he could find some new clients was well-founded. Archer spent a half hour chatting with Piers Prescott, Duke's college roommate. Prescott came from old money, but had the spirit of philanthropy one didn't often find in the private equity sector. Unfortunately he also had a good memory for names.

"Quinn, from San Francisco," said Piers thoughtfully. "Any relation to Ted Quinn, the venture capitalist?"

Archer was used to that question. In San Francisco, he'd heard it all the time. Quinntillion, his father's venture capital firm, was based there, and it was legendary in financial circles. Archer never used his full name, but any time someone discovered he was really Theodore Archer Quinn II, they would exclaim, "You must be Ted Quinn's son!" He'd moved to Boston partly to get away from it.

He took a breath and nodded. "He's my father."

"Well." Piers looked mildly impressed. "Quite a history."

He doubted the man meant Ted's personal history, the one that mattered to Archer. "He's a legend," he said evenly, not adding his personal qualifier: *and a legendary jerk.*

"I think my family firm did some business with him." Piers gave him a rueful glance. "If I recall, it was a bit bruising."

Archer raised his glass in mock salute. "That's the Quinn way. Sorry; I don't have anything to do with Quinntillion."

"No, I'm sure I would have remembered if Ted's son had been part of his firm," muttered Piers with a curiously grim expression.

Archer shook his head. "I went the other way. Computer science, then law. Which all worked out brilliantly when I crossed paths with Duke." He grinned. "We both rocked Master Chief."

Piers frowned, then groaned. "Don't say *Halo*. Duke wore out our Xbox on that game. I can still hear the Gregorian chant soundtrack, and it makes me break out in hives."

"Yep," said Archer proudly. "I won the campus tournament."

Piers eyed him. "How . . . impressive."

He laughed. "My crowning achievement!"

"What's that?" Duke had come up beside them. "Stealing my lawyer, Piers?"

"Another *Halo* warrior? Hardly."

Duke grinned. "Whatever. Hey, Archer, come meet Jane."

Piers moved off as Duke led him through the scattered guests to a pretty blond woman. Archer had seen her before, but he'd never actually met the future Mrs. Austen. She was friendly and pleasant, thanking him for coming to the wedding as if she really meant it, and it triggered something in Archer's memory.

"I wonder if I could ask a favor," he said to her. "My secretary Denise is a big fan of your books, and she sent one of them with me in the hopes you would sign it."

Jane's mouth opened in surprise, then she beamed.

"Of course! Which book?"

"Er." Archer cleared his throat. *"The Wicked Wallflower."*

An evil grin spread across Duke's face. "Oh, that's a good one. My favorite, in fact. That's the one where a man finds himself engaged without having to propose."

Jane gave him a look. "I would be thrilled to sign your book," she told Archer.

"It's for my secretary," Archer said again.

"Have you read the others?" Duke was enjoying this. "You don't want to miss any. *Wallflower Gone Wild* . . . whoa. I had to take a cold shower."

"Duke!" said Jane in exasperation.

"My secretary says you're her favorite author." Archer decided to ignore his client for a minute.

"She should be." Duke gave his future wife a scorching look. "Those books are badass."

Jane widened her eyes at him, but her smile ruined any reproof she might have meant. "You just made my night, Archer! Do you have the book?"

"Up in my room."

"Shall we go up? I don't want to forget and the next few days will be frantic."

They all walked up to his room. Archer pretended not to notice the whispered conversation between Duke and Jane, but he did catch a few heated glances between them. Duke had his arm around her waist and must have been whispering something dirty in her ear, from the way Jane was blushing.

While Jane sat down to autograph Denise's book, Duke prowled the room, glancing out each window. "Where do you run off to every day?"

"To get some work done. I can leave the office, but

it won't leave me."

"Right." Duke squinted into the sunset lighting up the west-facing windows. "Someone told me you found an Internet connection."

"Maybe."

His host's electric blue eyes flashed at him. "Where? I had to separate two programmers from each other's throats yesterday. They can't survive offline."

Archer shook his head with an air of regret. "I was sworn to secrecy. If I told you, I'd have to kill you."

Duke snorted. "Fine. Jane will be disappointed; she thought you were sneaking out to meet women, since you didn't bring a date."

For some completely unaccountable reason Archer found his throat needed clearing. Twice. "No. Just me and my laptop." Hidden away in Natalie's garden paradise, living for the little plates of sweets she brought out. He had a sudden memory of her rubbing one foot along the back of her other ankle, scribbling in her little notebook the whole while, and felt an unhealthy flush of heat suffuse his body.

"Your laptop makes you blush like a girl?" Duke grinned wickedly. "Don't forget I'm marrying a romance novelist. I know the signs, dude. I hope the woman you, ah, *aren't* sneaking out to see is a babe."

Archer was spared having to reply when Jane crossed the room to them. "Here you go." She handed Archer the book. "Tell your secretary I'm going to send her a copy of my next book before it comes out."

"She'll love that."

"Shall we go back down?" Duke draped his arm around Jane's shoulders. "Or not? I can't let one of my programmers get laid more often than I do at my own wedding."

"Oh my God, don't mention Rupert!" Jane groaned.

"How can I not?" returned Duke. "Is there a single person at this wedding who hasn't seen him and his girlfriend getting busy somewhere?"

Archer remembered the couple dry-humping out beyond the gazebo. "Are they the couple who can't keep their hands off each other?"

"I think they're sweet," said Jane sternly. "Just . . . indiscreet."

"Exhibitionists," muttered Duke to Archer.

"Well, maybe a little," agreed the bride, her face pink.

"So are we going back down?" Duke asked. Jane rolled her eyes at her fiancé, but went with him. At the door, Duke paused, glanced back at Archer, and hissed, "Ask her to the wedding."

"Who?" Archer tried to pretend he had no idea what Duke meant.

The groom smirked. "You know who."

The door closed behind them and Archer was left to contemplate it in silence. Ask Natalie to the wedding? He liked the idea, except that he didn't know her very well and had obviously said something wrong the last time they spoke. He wouldn't mind seeing her in a slinky dress, nor watching her walk around in high heels. He also wouldn't mind getting her out of the dress and heels, but he warned himself not to go there. And there had to be better place to take a woman than a wedding, where everyone would be drunk and prone to saying stupid things like, "When are you two getting married?" That was too much stress for any first date.

On the other hand . . . He was only in England for a few more days. Even though she was also from the Boston area, she might not be going back any time soon. Archer hesitated, then admitted to himself he would like to see much, much more of Natalie.

CHAPTER SIX

He walked down to the cottage the next morning and set up his laptop on the patio table as usual, but when he opened his e-mail, it failed to download. The internet indicator just blinked, indicating it wasn't finding a signal. Archer tried a few things, but still came up empty. The Wi-Fi was down.

Tentatively, he knocked on the garden door. After a minute the window opened and Natalie stuck out her head. "What?"

There was a streak of something dark on her cheekbone. Probably chocolate. The idea of licking it off popped into his brain, sudden and intense. He cleared his throat to get rid of the thought. "Uh, the, uh, the Wi-Fi seems to be out."

"Is it?" Something beeped behind her. "Shit!" She disappeared from the window.

Archer deliberated. He needed that Wi-Fi. He had also, unfortunately, sworn to stay out of her way, and it seemed clear there was a bit of chaos going on in the kitchen. While he stood there, she reappeared in the window. "Sorry about that, but I don't have time to fix it.

Maybe tonight." Another timer started beeping, and with a roll of her eyes she vanished again.

A whole day without access to his e-mail? Thanks to the last few days he wasn't behind, but he wasn't ahead, either; "out of the country" didn't translate into "unavailable for work" at Harper Millman. There was always the gazebo, he thought grimly. He could work with half the wedding party up there shouting into their phones, right?

He knocked again, then turned the knob and cautiously opened the door. As expected, it looked a bit out of control. No less than four pots steamed and bubbled atop the stove, and Natalie was stirring one, peering ferociously into the depths. "Maybe I could fix the Wi-Fi," he offered.

A timer beeped and she smacked one hand down on it, silencing it without a glance. "It's not my computer. It's kind of old and takes a good bit of cursing to get working."

"I'm pretty good with that type of machine."

Still stirring, she glanced at him. Her face was flushed pink and her hair was curling up over the scarf tied around her head. "They teach that in law school?"

"I was a computer science major before law school." He gave a hopeful grin. "I swear I won't break it."

She hesitated, and another timer went off. "Oh, fine, go ahead and try." She threw open the oven door and bent down to look inside. "Perfect," she breathed in apparent delight, lifting out a pan.

Archer unthinking agreed, blatantly staring at her ass, which was exquisitely displayed in a pair of faded jeans. "Absolutely."

Natalie looked up, stray curls falling around her

face. "What?"

He coughed, averting his eyes. "In there, you said?" He pointed at random.

"Yeah." Her attention switched back to the pan in her hands. "These are just right. Where's my pen?"

He left her making notes on whatever she'd baked, which smelled damned good, and went in search of the modem. She was right—it was an old machine, but it was also one he knew rather well. Back in college, he and his roommate had taken apart PCs like this for fun. Their room had looked like a factory exploded, but on the bright side, they built the most epic gaming system Harvard had ever seen.

The PC was set on an ornate desk that looked like something the Queen of France might have used. He followed the wires until he located the modem and other hardware, crammed into a large drawer in a squirrel's nest of cables and office supplies. What a mess. Whoever lived here had spent some good money on a very tasteful renovation of a really old house, then set up a computer system from the Dark Ages. Shaking his head, he pulled the drawer open and started unplugging things.

Natalie baked six perfect trays of madeleines before wondering what Archer was up to. A quick look at the clock revealed it was past one, which meant he'd been working on the computer . . . a really long time. He usually walked down the hill before nine. By now she was used to seeing him sitting out on the patio as she worked, and twice she'd caught herself glancing out the window before remembering why he wasn't there.

She made a few more notes on her madeleines and tossed her pen on the counter. Maybe it had been just a bit stupid to invite him to go fix the Wi-Fi. Who only knew what was on Amaryllis's creaky old computer, and now she'd just gone and let a complete stranger poke around it. The guy didn't seem dangerous or hacker-ish, but she had no basis for that. She pulled the scarf from her head and went into the office. "How's it going?" Then she looked around. "Oh my God, what did you do?"

"Don't worry," he said absently, his fingers flying across the keyboard. He had put two thick books on the Art Deco movement beneath the monitor to raise it up, and there was a jumble of cables and wires and electronic boxes in the middle of the floor. The drawer where everything usually went was open—and empty.

Natalie blanched. Pippa had told her not to mess with anything, that it was all a little touchy but should work as long as she didn't move things around. "This isn't my computer! I have to leave everything the way I found it."

He turned. "It's a miracle it worked at all the way it was. The modem cable was pinched in the drawer, and half this stuff doesn't work but was still plugged in. And when I started looking at the machine—"

"Whoa, why were you looking at the machine?" Shit; did Amaryllis have personal financial files on there? Nude photos? Given the hot young footballers she dated, it was a strong possibility. Natalie's heart lurched. Pippa would kill her. "Usually just unplugging the modem thing and plugging it back in works."

"Really?" He cast a skeptical eye on the discarded electronics. "That's a shock. No, I went to look at the software—nothing else," he added as if he could tell she was having an invasion-of-privacy freak-out. "The machine is all but crippled with malware. It's got a well-known virus that was slowing it down to glacial speed. Didn't you notice?"

Nope. "Well, I knew it was really old," she muttered in her own defense. "Old computers are always slow."

He grinned. "This one was beyond slow. It would drive me insane, so I started cleaning it up, and . . ." He checked his watch. "Time got away from me. Is it really after one?"

"Mmm-hmm." She nudged the tangle of stuff on the floor with one toe. "Please tell me you're going to put all this back together."

"Not on your life. Some of it's so old, there's no software to support it. I'll be glad to box it up for the owner, but he doesn't need any of it."

"She." Natalie gave the pile another worried look, then pushed the issue from her mind. She certainly wasn't going to go poking through, trying to figure out what everything was and how it might connect. A big note of apology to Amaryllis would have to suffice. "So is it working again?"

He turned back to the screen, where various status bars were inching forward. "Should be soon. It will be much faster once this is done."

"Well, that would be nice." Slowly she came across the room. "How does a computer science major end up a lawyer?"

"Change of heart, I guess."

She glanced sideways at him. There was more to it than that, from his carefully light tone. "Is that your connection to the wedding going on up there? It's some big technology guy getting married, right?"

His mouth quirked as if at some private joke.

"Maybe. But I'm here strictly for business reasons." He turned the chair around and gave her a rueful smile, the one that made him look young and almost bashful. "Would I be down here mooching off your Wi-Fi every day otherwise?"

"How would I know?" She opened her eyes wide. "Maybe you're a workaholic who doesn't even know how to have fun."

For a fraction of a second his eyes dropped. Not bashfully, but openly—though quickly—checking her out. "I hope that's not true."

Natalie opened her mouth, and nothing came out. Archer was a successful guy—smart, hardworking, funny, decent, and way too good-looking to be a real lawyer. It had been a long time since someone so obviously *right* checked her out. "So, no date for the wedding?" His eyebrows went up, and she hastily added, "I assume if you had a date, you'd be spending more time with her. Or him, as the case may be, because sometimes it is, you know, and that's fine."

His smile had started in the middle of her speech and grew as she rambled on. "If I had a date, she would no doubt be furious at me for working," he said, laying particular stress on the female pronoun. "But I haven't got a girlfriend, here or at home."

Thankfully something on the computer beeped, and he turned around again. Natalie took advantage of the moment to let her head drop back. *Smooth, girl,* she told herself. Not that she was hitting on him. She was just nosy. But she was also unreasonably pleased that he wasn't in a relationship. The more appealing he got, the more she'd thought he would be. Guys this *right* did not freely walk the earth.

"Here you are," Archer said, writing something on

a sticky note and pressing it down on the desk blotter. "The password was too easy and obvious; at least three other people have been freeloading on your system, and one of them seems to like porn."

"What?"

"Unless it's your thing," he said without missing a beat. "I'm not judging."

"I am not downloading porn!" Natalie wondered who the heck it was. Maybe Charles, the old duffer who came to work on the lawn and gardens every other week. She'd thought he was just reading a book, sitting on that bench beside the front door during his break. Hmm.

"Like I said, no judgment." Archer stood up and stretched his shoulders. He looked at the modem and router, now happily blinking little green lights. "Damn, I miss this," he said, almost to himself.

"Fixing computers from the dinosaur age?"

He flexed his fingers, snagging her gaze. He had really nice hands, she noticed again. "*Doing* something. Yeah, it's old, but when it was new, that was a top-of-the-line machine. I used to take those apart in college. My roommate and I were complete geeks; we booby-trapped the bathroom door down the hall with a little flashing light, and we wired a statue near our dorm with a speaker so we could spook tourists. I spent more time trying to write an AI essay generator than I spent writing actual essays, and nearly flunked an English class because of it. Still . . . It was fun."

"Why'd you give it up?" she asked softly.

The fondness of things remembered faded from his face. "Life changes."

That was the truth. Natalie wondered what had changed in his life to make him give up hacking his way around computers—maybe money? If he could afford to spend his college years taking apart "top-of-the-line machines," he must have had money—then. But now he spent his days hunched over a laptop looking beleaguered when he should have been on vacation, enjoying the wedding events.

"Right." She cleared her throat, suddenly wishing she wasn't wearing her worn-out jeans and a plain T-shirt. She shoved her hair from her forehead and cringed as her finger touched something gooey on her cheek. Not that she was hitting on Archer, or even interested in hitting on him. She turned back toward the kitchen, furtively swiping the gooey stuff from her face. "You want some lunch?"

Somehow Archer felt that being offered food again was a victory. He followed her into the kitchen, where she began pulling out plates. "I have roast chicken and coleslaw," she said. "Nothing very gourmet."

"Sounds great." He propped one shoulder against the doorway and watched as she fetched an armload of containers from the refrigerator. The dark smear on her cheek was wider and lighter now, as if she'd tried to wipe it away. "What are you baking today?"

She glanced up and flashed him a quick smile. "Madeleines. I also had a brain wave about ice cream overnight, even though I already did the ice creams, so I started a few custards as well."

"You're making ice cream?"

"Uh-huh. Did you think it was produced in a chemical factory somewhere?"

"No, I just didn't know anyone could make it at

home," he said. "It comes from the store in a box, like pasta."

She snorted and carved some slices off a fat loaf of crusty bread. "You can make pasta at home."

He whistled in quiet astonishment. "Maybe *you* can."

Natalie laughed, opening another container. "I am just as amazed that you could fix that old computer, so we're even. Rosemary mayo?"

Dumbly he nodded. Not only did it sound good, he was beginning to get a whiff of it. And there was something very sensual about the way she handled food. Her head tilted to the side as she swirled a dollop of mayonnaise onto the bread, then laid some tomato slices and lettuce on top of it. The blade of her knife glinted as she ran it through a whole chicken breast, the skin dark chestnut and speckled with herbs or spices or something. One by one she layered the sliced chicken on the bread before bringing the knife down through the sandwich, cutting it into halves. He had a strong feeling she'd made everything from scratch, and when he asked, she confirmed it.

"Of course. I'm writing a cookbook, remember."

"With recipes for mayonnaise and bread?"

She laughed again. "No, although they're both easy to make. I want my cookbook to be the sort of thing people turn to every night, not only for basics like a quick roasted chicken, but for dinner parties and special occasion meals. I start with easy, basic recipes, then add on layers of extras or different flavor variations. Most people don't have time to make mayonnaise, although . . ." She gave him a secretive little smile that made his stomach tighten. "I did include one recipe for how to flavor mayonnaise from the jar. A few chopped herbs and a squirt of lemon juice make a huge impact." She scooped out some coleslaw onto both plates, set a sandwich half on each, and handed him one. "Let's eat."

Archer was only too happy to obey.

"So when does the cookbook come out?" he asked as they ate on the patio. He'd pushed his laptop aside and now Oliver the cat lay on top of it. Archer barely glanced at it, fully diverted by the succulent sandwich in his hands and the fascinating woman across from him.

She took her time answering. "I don't know. I have to finish writing it."

He nodded. "Is the publisher getting impatient for it?" One of his clients had written a book on a computer language once, and Archer had helped him find a literary attorney for the book contract.

Natalie played with her coleslaw, chewing very slowly. Too late, Archer recognized the signs of someone who didn't want to answer. "That's not really my business. Never mind."

"No, it's okay." She took a deep breath. "I don't have a publisher yet. Writing a cookbook was . . . Well, it was an excuse to get out of Wellesley. My brother and I had a big fight about our family restaurant and I needed to get away."

He just listened.

"This house belongs to my college roommate's stepmother," she went on. "When I told Pippa I needed a hideout, she offered it."

He glanced at the house. One never knew what real estate was worth, but someone had spent a lot of money renovating this house. "Pretty nice hideout, if you ask me."

She smiled, a little pensive. "Very nice." She seemed to rouse herself from whatever had dampened her mood. "So you just moved to Boston?"

"From San Francisco. But I went to college in the Boston area and liked it. Still do."

"You moved back for work?"

He winked. "An offer I couldn't refuse."

"Something that combines computers and law," she guessed. "I have a guess whose wedding it is up there. The shop in town only sells trashy newspapers and they are full of rumors about Internet millionaires."

Archer pushed back his plate and heaved a happy, sated, sigh. "I don't do the computers anymore, just the law. But being able to speak the language helps with my clients, who include"—he tapped one temple—"many very successful Internet entrepreneurs."

"Oh?" She raised one eyebrow teasingly. "So it's no one famous getting married?"

He made a stern face. "I can't really discuss it. Client confidentiality, you know."

One side of her mouth curled upward, giving her a sly, sexy look. "Got it." She folded her arms and rested her elbows on the table. "Why not computers? You said you miss it."

It was his turn to take a moment before answering. "I loved it," he finally said, slowly. "I got my degree in computer science and did a couple of years as a programmer. I wasn't brilliant," he added, "just generally competent and brash as heck." Duke Austen had hacked the *New York Times* front page as a middle-schooler before channeling his intellect into more socially acceptable—and profitable—directions. Archer had been a very competent mid-level programmer, who would have written search engine algorithms forever if he'd stayed.

She ran her finger along the edge of her plate,

picking up a bit of mayo. She stuck out her tongue and delicately licked it off her fingertip. Archer stared, feeling the stirrings of a very different sort of hunger. Every time he saw Natalie, he liked her more and more. Damn Duke and his suggestion of asking her to be his date to the wedding.

"Why law?" It seemed her voice had grown throaty and seductive with that lick of mayo.

He hesitated. "Because of my father."

"Oh." She tilted her head to one side, obviously picking up on his discomfort. "My mother runs the kitchen in our restaurant. I'm following in her footsteps, too."

Archer gave a sharp laugh. "My father's not a lawyer. He told my mother he was divorcing her three weeks after she was diagnosed with breast cancer. She's so tenderhearted, she told him to go—her cancer was pretty advanced and I think she didn't expect to survive. But I could have killed him. He'd been banging his assistant for some time, but to leave Mum at that moment . . ." He shook his head. "I had a friend whose mother did divorce law, and she turned out to be a real shark. Thanks to her, my mother ended up with a good settlement and guaranteed lifetime health insurance. I was impressed. I wasn't really hitting it out of the park as a programmer, so I decided to go into law." He shrugged. "Divorce law didn't do it for me, but corporate law did, and not many attorneys really know their way around tech clients. So that's my specialty."

Her face had grown soft and compassionate during his story. "How's your mother doing now?"

"Quite well. She got an experimental drug in a clinical trial and it beat back the tumor. She gardens, she paints, she bakes . . ." He forced a grin. "If living with my father for twenty years didn't kill her, cancer seemed unlikely to."

"Ah. Still haven't forgiven him?" She sounded understanding.

His jaw clenched. "No." Not forgiven, nor spoken to in years, and Archer was very happy to keep it that way. Ted Quinn was a heartless bastard. He'd been an absent father and an indifferent husband, and Archer didn't care if they never saw each other again.

For a few moments all was quiet. Natalie drew circles in the remnants of her coleslaw with her fork. "I still haven't forgiven my brother, either. He's actually the reason I left. I take it your father is in San Francisco?" Surprised, he nodded once. "My brother followed my father into the restaurant administrative side. I cooked, Paul learned accounting. But Paul wants to turn the restaurant into a chain, with locations around the country, and I just . . ." She huffed in controlled temper. "I think he's wrong. It will ruin what's special about us."

"Which is?" He leaned forward. The sun was on her hair, giving her a halo of reddish curls. That smear of chocolate was still on her cheek, and he couldn't stop staring at it.

"It's called Cuisine du Jude, after my mother Judy. We made the big time with a review in the *New York Times* restaurant section, calling it the most perfect date night . . ."

"Date night restaurant in America," he finished with her. "I've heard of it! Wow."

"Ever been there?" she asked.

"Nope. Couldn't get a table." He shook his head in amazement. "The managing partner at my firm, Jack Harper, takes his wife there every anniversary. I overheard his secretary making next year's booking before I left—for

March."

"Oh, good." She beamed in pleasure. "I love being part of someone's anniversary tradition!"

Archer's lungs seized up. Oh hell; she was something when she smiled. It lit up her face and made her eyes sparkle.

"Well." Natalie pushed her chair back. "I'd better get back to custards, and you've spent all morning fixing that old computer. Thanks for doing that, by the way."

"My pleasure," he said, still mesmerized.

She picked up the plates and went back into the kitchen. Archer seized the glasses and followed. Inside, she was scraping the plates over the sink, and moved aside as he put the glasses on the drainboard. "Thanks," she said again, looking up at him with a smile.

Archer stared at her. Slowly her smile faded, and the same awareness he felt prickling beneath his skin seemed to affect her. "What?" she said in that throaty voice. "Have I got something on my face?"

"You do, actually." He raised one hand and ran his thumb over the dark smear. Her breathing hitched, but she didn't move. Even more slowly, he repeated the motion. "I think it's dried chocolate," he murmured.

A wash of faint pink came into her cheeks. "Probably. I was making chocolate custard earlier . . ."

His mouth crooked up. Of course. "My favorite."

"I thought chocolate cake was your favorite," she breathed, not making any motion to retreat as he angled his head closer to hers.

"Chocolate is my favorite." He brushed his lips against hers. "And this." He kissed her, lightly, his fingertips barely touching the bottom of her chin. Hesitantly her lips moved against his, and then her fingers wrapped around a fold of his shirt and pulled. Archer didn't waste a moment; his fingers slid around the nape of her neck and he drew her against him with his other arm.

He'd thought she smelled good; she tasted even better. Her mouth opened under his and she tasted of rosemary and, faintly, of chocolate, and he thought he'd never get enough. Her fingers flexed, gripping his shirt even tighter, and she rose up on her toes, kissing him back. Her tongue met his, hot and bold, and Archer felt the ground give way beneath his feet. He could kiss this woman forever.

She gave an audible gasp when he broke the kiss so he could taste more of her skin. "I don't even know you." Her voice was that husky whisper that drove him wild.

"I know." Nor did he know her, but he meant to remedy that. His lips brushed the chocolate smear on her cheek and he had a sudden image of licking chocolate off every part of her.

"This is really fast."

"I know," he said again, nipping her earlobe between his teeth. Fast and hot and more intense than anything he'd ever felt in his life.

A fine shudder went through her. "But it feels so damn good . . . Are you sure you don't have a girlfriend?"

"Completely unattached." He kissed her jaw. "You?"

She gave a faint shake of her head, which exposed her neck better to his kisses. "No one."

"Do you want me to stop?"

For a moment she was motionless, then another very tiny shake of her head. "No."

He smiled, his mouth against hers again. "Good." He held her tighter, and reveled in the feel of her body moving against his. It was shocking how badly he wanted her—he'd gone from intending a one-time kiss, exploratory and romantic, to crowding her against the door and fending off the driving urge to slip his hand up her shirt and hike her legs around his waist and . . .

Something buzzed. Archer ignored it, but Natalie jumped. "Archer," she said in a shaky voice. "Your phone is ringing."

"It does that a lot." Reluctantly, he let go of her. It felt like molten lava flowed beneath his skin, slow and thick and scorching. Natalie's face was flushed and her eyes were bright, but she turned her head and stared at the far wall of the kitchen. He took a step back to keep from kissing her again, and pulled the phone from his pocket. It was Duke Austen, and he silently cursed his VIP client's shitty timing as he answered the call. "Hey, Duke."

"Bad news," said Austen grimly. "Some tabloid dick seems to have gotten wind of the locale, which is going to screw up the magazine deal. Jane is really upset."

Archer said a few more curses inside his head. If a tabloid published wedding photos first, the magazine deal was off—along with any hope the couple had of having a private wedding. Brampton House would be crawling with paparazzi within a few hours if word got out, no matter how many security firms were hired to keep them away. "Are you sure? Has he published?"

"I don't know." Duke's voice seethed with anger. "What can we do?"

He sighed. This wasn't his area of expertise, but Duke was his client. He gave Natalie an apologetic glance and stepped away. She gave a jerky nod and began making a clatter with dishes in the sink. Archer lowered his voice. "Let me make some calls. I'll get back to you."

"Where are you?" demanded Duke.

"On my way back to the hotel. Give me twenty minutes." He ended the call. Natalie was still washing dishes, scrubbing energetically. "I have to go," he said quietly.

She nodded, her curls bouncing. "Okay."

He stepped up behind her and laid his hands on her hips. A muscle tensed in her waist, but she didn't look at him. "I don't want to."

"Well." She inhaled deeply as he pressed his lips to the back of her neck. "Can't always do what you want to . . ."

Wasn't that the truth. He wanted to stay right here, exploring the velvety skin at her nape, breathing the intoxicating tropical smell of her skin, kissing his way along the slope of her collarbone. He wanted to throw gasoline on the sparks that smoldered between them and walk into the blaze. For a lingering moment he ignored the call of duty; he refused to think about how many calls he'd have to make to solve Duke's problem.

Natalie took a long, shuddering breath and twisted around in his arms. Her hands landed flat on his chest. "Archer—"

"Don't tell me it's too fast unless you want it to stop now," he whispered, tucking her against him once more. "Do you?"

Her gaze dropped. "Not at the moment . . ."

"Good. Neither do I." He kissed her again, hard and hungrily. "I'll see you tomorrow."

Looking dazed, she nodded. He bent his head and licked the chocolate off her cheek. "My favorite," he breathed again, right next to her ear. She gave a soft moan, and he made himself let go of her and walk away without looking back.

CHAPTER SEVEN

Natalie scrubbed at the dishes until they would have passed muster at the White House. Her skin felt electrified, and she did not want to think about how close she'd come to having sex with a man she'd only met four days ago, up against the kitchen pantry door.

She swiped at the chocolate on her face again. *You don't have to shag him,* echoed her mother's voice in her head. *Yeah, but what if I want to?* she silently retorted. Her mother had probably said that only because Natalie was definitely not the type who would. Even in college she'd never gotten serious with a guy within the first month. Now she was so turned on by one kiss from Archer, if he'd made any move to take things further she would have dragged him into the other room and started tearing off her clothes.

"Okay," she said aloud, horrified by the breathless tenor of her voice. "Okay. You're a little deprived." Although she hadn't felt so bothered by that yesterday. "It's just hot when a guy comes on to you like that." So hot, her knees were still shaking. "Get over it, Nat."

Her phone shrilled loudly then, and she nearly dropped the glass she was washing for the fourth time. Her heart leapt into her throat. Archer? But no—he didn't even have her phone number, and when she seized the phone, it was Pippa's ID on the screen. Taking a deep breath and telling herself it was relief and not disappointment, she answered. "Hi."

"Are you still terribly oppressed by the traffic?" said her friend in greeting. "I've been feeling just awful for telling you it would be quiet."

"Oh . . . I'm surviving."

"Are you sure? Because I'm willing to trade you, my flat in Hammersmith for the cottage. The kitchen's not as big, but I'm a rotten friend for sending you into a construction zone when you only asked for peace and quiet. I can drive out tonight and help you move."

"No, don't," she mumbled. Archer was only here for a wedding, which meant he'd be gone in a week or so. That already sounded short.

There was silence on the phone, almost palpably curious. "Are they done, then? I thought you were ready to detonate the road to put an end to it."

"I got used to it, I guess . . ."

"Natalie," said Pippa carefully, "are you okay? You sound stoned."

She let her head fall back. "I'm not stoned." She paused. "I have a serious case of lust for one of the guys attending the wedding at Brampton House," she said in a rush, almost hearing Pippa's mouth drop open. "I just kissed him. And made out with him."

There was a long silence, then Pippa said in her most proper, bossy voice, "Put the real Natalie back on the line, please."

"I know! Totally not like me! But I did, and Pip"— she lowered her voice to a whisper even though only Oliver the cat would hear her—"I would have done more."

"Oh my God, was he not into you?" demanded Pippa. "Boot his ass out the door."

"No, his phone rang." She looked out the window, but Archer was long gone. Oliver sprawled on the table where he usually worked. "I think it was work. He works a lot."

"Details," commanded Pippa.

Natalie obliged. Not that she knew much about him, as was blindingly clear from the brevity of her explanation. "He said he'd see me tomorrow," she finished. "What do you think: should I have sex with him or not?"

Her friend snorted with laughter. "You're absolutely gagging for it! I say sex. Lord knows I never saw anyone worth shagging in Melbury; hot men are like the Loch Ness monster around there."

"Not this week. I've seen people who must be wedding guests. More than one has been hot."

Pippa swore. "You would find the one week in eternity when there are attractive men in town. I lived there for *two years*, Nat, and saw nary a one."

"You only spent summers here."

"Two endless summers without so much as a buff delivery man. Carpe diem."

Natalie rubbed her toes down the back of her leg. "You don't think he's just looking to hook up because that's what people do at weddings?"

"Natalie," said Pippa with great patience, "who cares? You want to shag him; if he wants to shag you, where is the problem?"

"You are the worst conscience a girl could ever have," she told her friend.

Pippa laughed. "I'm the evil genie on your shoulder,

not your conscience! Look him up online to satisfy your nerves, then put on that red dress you have and wear nothing underneath."

"I didn't even bring that dress!"

"Then wear any old skirt. If he wants you, he won't notice anyway."

"Good-bye, Pip." She hung up and put down the phone. Pippa was wilder than she was—although the very fact that Natalie was considering sleeping with Archer, after only one kiss and zero dates, hardly left her feeling more virtuous. Still . . .

She went into the other room, averting her eyes from the pile of discarded electronics on the floor. She opened the browser and typed in Archer's name in the search bar. And she learned . . . He was a lawyer. The first several pages of results were all legal related, although they did load much faster than usual, as he'd promised. She clicked the images tab, and the screen filled with his face, giving her another little jolt of attraction. They were mostly professional photos, but one caught her eye and she clicked it. It was Archer, several years younger, with an older man who had to be his father. The resemblance was unmistakable. *Ted Quinn of Quintillion Capital and Archer Quinn of Scarsdale Phillips LLP,* was the caption; it had been taken at a charity event in San Francisco. Natalie's gaze lingered on Archer's face. He was smiling, but it was almost grim and forced. His father's smile, on the other hand, was straight out of a mouthwash commercial. Archer said he hadn't forgiven his dad even years after the divorce. In fact, it sounded like he still hated his father. That sounded . . . implacable. Rigid, even.

With a shake of her head, she went back to her original search. She was only contemplating a brief fling. It didn't really matter what his family relations were like because she would probably never meet them. She only cared that he wasn't a crazy person, now that he knew about her family restaurant and could find her again, and the Internet was hardly likely to tell her much about that. The only thing to do was put some form of restraint on her hormones and try to get to know the guy. She closed the browser and went back to the kitchen, even though she had very little interest in custards or madeleines anymore.

Duke's problem did not turn out to be easily fixed. A handful of photos, allegedly of Jane in her wedding dress, had ended up online, and the magazine was threatening to jettison the charity deal. Duke was in a fury, although he had to back down a bit when Archer discovered the maid of honor had posted the photos—and that her date was the publisher of several tabloid newspapers.

"You invited Damien Knightly, owner of *The London Weekly?*" he asked incredulously. "Duke—no offense—but what were you thinking? Did you make him sign a nondisclosure agreement?"

Duke scowled. "No. But I know he's behind these photos. Roxanna wouldn't do this to Jane on her own."

Archer exhaled and paced around the room. "I wish you'd mentioned this earlier." He raised his hand in appeasement as his client scowled harder. "How bad are the pictures?"

"Fugly as hell," said Duke. "Can I shoot the guy? We're going hunting tomorrow."

"Please don't." Archer winced.

"Whatever. Maybe I can get Compton to shoot

him; it's his property. But Knightly's not the only problem; there's a sleazy freelance photographer also lurking about. Jane was in tears over the deal falling apart, and I admit it's been kind of nice not having my every action on TMZ." He made a face. "I thought the attention would go away, now that I'm settling down."

Archer gave him a look. "Seems like not. I'll call Tom and have him get in touch with the magazine people, expressing your outrage over the suggestion that you've violated the deal and reaffirming your commitment to it. Can I say the photos are probably frauds?"

"Whatever it takes," said Duke moodily. "I just don't want someone watching us from behind every tree."

"I understand." He already had his phone in hand to look up the number for Tom Kincaid, the entertainment attorney at his firm who'd done the magazine deal. Archer didn't know much about that area of law, but Duke was his client and it was his responsibility to see that it was fixed.

"Thanks, dude."

Archer went back to his room. This wasn't a call he could place from the top of the hill, where anyone might overhear what was confidential and potentially very costly. And if he walked back to Natalie's garden, he wasn't sure he'd be able to keep his full attention on the question at hand. She'd looked unbelievably sexy when he left, her face flushed and her hair rumpled and her eyes dilated with desire. If Duke hadn't called him, Archer wasn't sure they wouldn't have ended up naked. He felt like he was being swept away by an avalanche; the first step had seemed small and fairly innocent, but now he was almost in free fall. He couldn't wait to see her again. He was dying to kiss her again. He reached for the landline to call Tom, hoping his colleague would find a quick solution.

But there wasn't one, and he ended up on a conference call with Tom and the magazine lawyers. Archer foresaw his evening slipping away. He looked longingly out the window toward Natalie's cottage. It was hidden from sight, but if he closed his eyes he could still picture her leaning against the pantry door, head back, throat exposed all the way down to the so-tempting valley between her breasts. Damn it. He was almost ready to make the charity payment himself, just to be done with this so he could go back to Primrose Cottage.

Duke knocked on his door at one point, in search of an update, and Archer could only give a tentative thumbs-up. He'd boldly claimed the dress photos were fake, and while the magazine lawyers weren't completely convinced, it had given them pause. After some haggling, Tom got them to agree that they wouldn't exercise the termination clause until after the wedding, when they would have their own unquestionably authentic photos to compare to these blurry shots. Duke readily agreed to hire more security to prevent any more lapses, and vowed to remind all guests that they were not to post photos online.

Finally the magazine lawyers said they would confer and get back to them. Tom promised to stay on it, and Archer hung up the phone in relief. Duke slapped his shoulder in gratitude, and invited him to come have a drink with him and Jane. Curious to know why Jane hadn't kicked out her maid of honor, Archer went, but Jane only thanked him effusively before being swept away by a tall redhead, who turned out to be that maid of honor, Roxanna Lane. So she was the one who'd brought the tabloids right into the wedding party and nearly ruined the magazine deal? Archer watched her for a few minutes, until a guy in an expensive suit came and put his arm around her waist. That must be Damien Knightly. Duke had said Jane was in tears over the possible breached deal, but she was chatting amiably enough with Roxanna and Knightly now.

Well. Let Duke sort that out. Archer had more important things to think about now, like the next time he could see Natalie. Fast, she'd called it. He knew that, but didn't want to change anything. At the moment he was completely willing to let himself be swept away by the avalanche. But he also didn't want to end up a broken, bruised mess when it stopped, which meant he had to back up a step. Slow things down, just a tiny bit, without sacrificing any of the heat between them.

He needed a plan. And the way to a chef's heart . . . had to include chocolate.

CHAPTER EIGHT

Natalie had barely come downstairs the next morning when Archer tapped on the kitchen door. She pushed it open, unable to stop the smile that spread across her face as he presented her with a small posy of flowers.

"Good morning," he said.

"Thank you." She held them to her nose before plopping them into the sink. "That's a nice way to start the day."

"I can think of one better."

Her toes curled in her slippers. Without hesitation she raised her face, inviting him to kiss her. He did so at once, his hand molding around the back of her neck to pull her to him. Just as Natalie began to list toward him, forgetting every bit of her overnight resolution to be more circumspect and get to know him, he lifted his head. Saving her from herself, she thought.

"And I brought breakfast." He held up a paper bag. "Stole it from the kitchen. The chef up at the hotel is a real prick, but he can cook."

She pushed the door closed. "How nice it will be to eat something other than my own cooking!"

"I thought as much." He pointed at a cabinet with a questioning look, and she nodded; plates were in there, along with coffee cups. She started the coffee as he took some pastries out of the paper bag. "I also thought it was fair, after you fed me yesterday, that I feed you. My first thought was dinner, but then someone at my office scheduled me on a call for dinnertime." He made a noise of disgust. "So I thought of lunch . . . until the concierge informed me there are only two decent places to eat locally: the village pub and a vegan restaurant called The Pineapple of Perfection."

Natalie began to laugh at the aggrieved expression on his face.

"I grew up in San Francisco," he argued. "I have nothing against vegan food, and sometimes it's quite good. Sometimes . . . It's seaweed." He shuddered. "And that left breakfast."

"Breakfast is my favorite meal of the day," she told him, still laughing. "Thank you."

"Really?" His eyes heated and skimmed down her body. "It might be mine too."

"Because of coffee?" She rested her elbows on the counter and cocked her head, feeling sexy and flirty. She wore her cutoff denim skirt, the one that ended well above her knees, and a long-sleeve shirt that was tight and stretchy with a deep V in front. It was not cooking attire. But as Archer's gaze slid right down to her breasts, it felt like the giant AGA had been on for hours.

"Coffee," he murmured distractedly, "and other things."

"Such as?" God, Pippa would cheer if she could hear how throaty Natalie's voice had gone. Even to her own ears she sounded like a phone sex operator.

He lifted his gaze back to her face. "Such as doing something right. Not rushing it."

"Were you rushing it yesterday?"

He shook his head slowly, his eyes fixed on her. "But I don't want to risk anything."

Her cheeks warmed. "You're doing fine so far."

One corner of his mouth curled upward. "Thought so."

Thankfully the coffee machine beeped, and she busied herself with it. Was there anything wrong with him? Most guys she dated were happy to let her cook for them, including serving. Archer moved around the kitchen as she fixed the coffee, finding napkins and even a vase for the flowers. By the time she had the cappuccino prepared, he had set the table, complete with bouquet, and stood waiting to pull out her chair. It felt so comfortable, so *right,* she almost didn't know what to say.

"Chivalry," she joked lamely, letting him seat her. His fingers ran over her shoulders and lingered at her nape for just a moment, but it was enough to send a thrill down her spine.

He took the seat next to hers. "My mother told me it would make an impression."

"She gives good advice." Natalie studied the selection of pastries. "But then, making an excellent chocolate pudding cake is already a sterling recommendation."

"I quite agree. And speaking of that—" He fished a folded paper from his shirt pocket. "I got it. My gift to you, as no cookbook should be without chocolate pudding cake."

She unfolded it and read the printout of a scanned, handwritten recipe. His mother had elegant handwriting, and she made very careful and exact notes about how to melt the chocolate and how to tell when the cake was done. Natalie was impressed. "It looks delicious."

"You can tell from reading the recipe?" He bit into a large frosted bun.

Natalie selected a sticky roll covered with finely chopped nuts. "Somewhat." She took a bite and closed her eyes. It *was* good. "Just like I bet you can tell from reading a contract if something's a good deal."

His eyes had riveted on her mouth as she ate. "Yeah," he murmured. "Usually."

She ran her tongue over her lower lip, turned on by the way he watched her do it. "I hope your mom didn't mind you giving it away."

"Not at all." His lazy grin reappeared. "Better that than I try to make it myself."

"It doesn't look that complicated."

"Maybe not," he replied, "but it needs to be done just right. When it is . . ." He put his fingers to his lips. "Heaven." He carried the kiss to her hand, lying on the table. "When it's not . . ." He shrugged, swirling his fingers over her hand. "Crap."

"Now I don't know if I can ever make it," she said unevenly, mesmerized as his fingers moved up her wrist to play with the sleeve of her shirt. "The pressure . . ."

"Mmm, you'll rise to the occasion," he whispered. "Lick your lip."

"Why?"

"You've got something sticky on your upper lip, and if you don't lick it off, I will."

She stared at him. Then she reached out, dragged her finger through the frosting on his half-consumed bun, and smeared it on her lip. Archer let out his breath. "I was hoping you'd do that," he said before pushing his chair back and hauling her into his lap. Natalie's short skirt rode up around her hips as she straddled his thighs and he cupped both hands around her head for a scorching kiss. She slid her arms around his neck and stomped any lingering voice of hesitation into silence. It wasn't too fast if she wanted him as desperately as he wanted her. It didn't matter that she hadn't known him since nursery school, not when everything was just so *right* with him.

"Damn." He pulled back, breathing hard. "I keep losing my train of thought around you. You said two things yesterday. One, that this was going very fast, and two, that you don't know me." He paused to brush his lips against hers again, then looked her right in the eyes. "I don't feel inclined to change the first, but I can change the second." He settled her more comfortably on his lap. Something inside her quaked as his hard-on pressed against her thigh, but aside from a brief catch in his breathing, Archer didn't acknowledge it.

"Let's see . . . My birthday is August fourteenth. I tend to get a little crazy about San Francisco Giants baseball, but not other sports. My real first name is Theodore." She raised her brows and grinned, and he gave her a stern look. "Don't you dare use it. It's my dad's name. My mother is named Patricia and she lives in Sonoma wine country. It's beautiful out there, you'll love it."

Natalie ignored the way her heart jolted at the veiled suggestion she might ever visit his mother. "Is that where you grew up?"

He shook his head. "San Francisco. My father's firm is there and we lived in the city."

She ran her finger down his collar. "What is venture capital?"

Very subtly, he tensed. "Investment money."

"And that's what your dad does?"

His eyes grew dark and for a moment she thought she'd crossed a line. "Yes."

Natalie bit her lip but forged on. "You said you hadn't forgiven him, but it sounds like the divorce was a while ago. I only had the blowout with my brother a few weeks ago and I don't think I could endure being angry at him for years. It just struck me as . . . Well, as odd that you haven't spoken to your dad in forever."

For a minute he didn't answer. "My dad's a hard man, Natalie. I don't hate him, but I don't really like him, either. I don't care that he divorced Mum; he was a rotten husband anyway. But he made her feel like shit when he did it, and you know what? He's very good at that. He's a manipulator and a snake oil salesman who always covers his own ass and is more than willing to throw other people under the bus. On the other hand . . ." He ran one hand up her bare thigh. "I think you and your brother are on the same team, when the going gets tough, and that you actually like him. My dad is only on his team, and he's only likable when he wants something from you."

She nodded. That was fair; not every parent was admirable and worthy of respect. And Archer was right about her and Paul, despite the feud between them now. She was still angry at her brother, but not as much as when she'd left. "I have another nosy question," she said, changing the subject. "Why haven't you got a girlfriend?"

He leaned back, his eyes glittering at her. "I work a lot."

"So you haven't got time for anyone?"

"No, I haven't got time to meet anyone." His gaze dipped to the V of her shirt. "Usually." Without thinking she subtly arched her back, and his breath caught again. "And when I hadn't met anyone, there was no reason to blow off work . . . It's a vicious cycle."

"You should try working in a restaurant," she said lightly. "I'm free between two and four, then again after midnight."

"So if I ask you out for coffee at three, you'll be available?"

"Are you asking?" she asked coyly, batting her eyelashes and trying not to blush while she hoped he said *yes.*

"Just checking." His hands had relocated to her hips, just above where her skirt was bunched up. "Anything else you'd like to know?"

She could ask anything, she realized; he was telling her without asking similar questions in return. He was also enormously aroused, yet hadn't made a move, even though the thought had crossed her mind—more than once—that if she took off her underwear, they could have sex right here and now on this chair. But he wanted to get to know her. He'd brought her food and flowers, which counted as a proper date. Pippa had said it didn't matter if he only wanted a wedding hookup, but if it turned out he wanted more . . . something like a real relationship . . .

"So you don't have to work today?" she asked, feeling reckless and a bit wild.

His smile was edged with promise. "Today I am blowing off work. Today we're going to have fun."

Archer returned to Brampton House in a buoyant mood.

After breakfast, he and Natalie had walked into the village. They bought sandwiches and a bottle of wine at the tiny gourmet shop and ate a picnic lunch on the grass in a nearby park. He told her about the wedding, including the grouse-hunting bachelor party he had skipped that morning, and she told him about her family's restaurant, like the time a diner wanted to propose and put the engagement ring in the frosting atop his girlfriend's cake, but didn't pop the question before she ate it, ring and all. Natalie had decided to get a cat, based on her time with Oliver, and Archer regaled her with stories of his mother's various cats until she laughed so hard she cried. She teased him about his love of dessert by describing the cakes she'd baked recently, which were all stored in Primrose Cottage's walk-in wine cooler. He was entranced. When his phone buzzed with a reminder of his business call, he was astonished to realize they had talked all day. He walked her home and said good-bye with a kiss so hot, he very nearly forgot that he had to leave.

He jogged up the stairs to his room, finally beginning to wonder what Jack wanted to talk about. His boss had e-mailed the previous night to set it up and had only said it was in regard to funding for Brightball. Archer had almost stopped thinking about that client entirely, between Duke's tabloid trouble and Natalie. But if Brightball finally had some funding, Jack would probably want him to revise the financing documents. For once Archer planned to defer it. He could work on the plane home, but until then he was going to keep having fun.

After the warm day outside, his hotel room felt lonely and dark. There was no smell of chocolate baking, and he couldn't see Primrose Cottage. He even missed Oliver the cat jumping up and trying to lie on his keyboard.

With no Wi-Fi, he could only review the notes and documents he'd already downloaded to his laptop, catch up on his billing, and wait for Jack.

The call was almost a half hour late. Sunk in thought, watching clouds drift across the twilight sky as he wondered if Natalie would still be awake after this call ended, Archer jumped when the phone on his desk rang, the muted trill loud in the quiet room.

"Archer," boomed Jack's voice over the line. "Hope we aren't keeping you from the bachelor party or anything."

"I wouldn't skip that for you," he said. Just for Natalie.

The other man laughed. "That's right, you're on vacation."

Archer cast a jaundiced eye at the billing worksheet open on his laptop. He'd logged over thirty-five hours since setting foot on English soil. Some vacation—aside from Natalie's cooking, anyway. "If you say so. Is Bill there?"

"Hi Archer," piped up Bill, his voice vibrating with suppressed eagerness. "Big day, huh?"

"No, the wedding is this weekend." But somehow he knew Bill wasn't asking about the wedding.

Bill just laughed.

"The good news is that we've got a funding offer," said Jack. "A fantastic one. We've been working out details with the investors this week. I'll let them introduce themselves, but I set up this call to hammer out the main terms. Hold on a moment and I'll get them on the line."

Archer raised his eyebrows, doodling a string of dollar signs and a large question mark on his notebook. Who was this investor? Brightball had enormous potential, but so far had fallen short on convincing the venture funds to chip in more than a pittance.

"Hey there, I'm Rick Garner," said a new voice. The name rang a bell, but Archer couldn't put his finger on it. "Glad to join you all; I'm looking forward to working with everyone. I'll be the point person on Brightball."

"Good morning," said a voice with a faint German accent. "Dietrich Metzer here."

Well, shit. The bell rang crystal clear this time, even before Rick Garner added, "And our principal will be sitting in on the call today."

"Good morning, gentlemen. Hello, Archer," came a rich, genial voice. It was a movie star voice, the kind of voice hired to record commercials for expensive luxury cars. It was a compelling voice, one that could persuade you to pay ten percent above your absolute price ceiling and still make you feel like you got a bargain. It was a voice that could tell a woman with third-stage breast cancer that she was being divorced, and make her think everything was her fault.

Archer flung his pencil at the wall, not caring that it left a black dot on the wallpaper. "Hello, Dad."

"Nice of you to join us, Mr. Quinn," said Jack.

"Quinntillion is investing twenty-seven million in the company," piped up Bill, sounding far too pleased with himself.

Archer smiled grimly. So this was what had got Bill so excited. Too bad he had no idea what he'd gotten himself into. "When did this come about?"

"All in the last week. Jack led the negotiations." Bill paused. "I thought he would let you know."

"Archer's overseas at the moment," said Jack quickly. "What with the time difference and all, I just hadn't found time to bring him up to speed."

"No sweat. Well, as you can imagine we've got quite a bit of stuff to talk about . . ." And Bill plunged into the terms of the new investment. Archer let Jack do most of the talking, just as he intended to let Jack do most of the work. This was obviously Jack's doing; if he'd wanted Archer's input, he would have asked for it days ago, before Bill became enamored of the idea of Quinntillion money. Ted Quinn was reputed to have the golden touch, after all, and when he invested, he invested big. That didn't mean he didn't get something for his money, though; Ted always demanded what he valued most, which was control. No doubt Bill had barely thought past all the ways he could use Quintillion's money. The full extent of the devil's bargain he'd made wouldn't dawn on him until much later, when he found himself eased out the door of the company that was his entire life.

When the call finally ended, Archer hung up, counted to ten, and dialed Jack's number. "It must be my birthday," he said in false delight. "You forgot to jump up and shout, 'Surprise!'"

Jack's sigh echoed across the Atlantic. "I wasn't keeping it from you. You've just been hard to reach, and I wanted to tell you myself."

"On the phone with our client listening? Your presentation skills need work."

"You've been gone almost a week," retorted Jack.

"That doesn't mean I haven't been working, and I don't just mean socializing with our firm's other clients, as you strongly encouraged me to do." They both knew Project-TK meant far more to their bottom line than Brightball, at least for the moment.

"To be honest, Archer, I didn't think I would be the one to get Quinntillion involved in a deal with any of our clients."

Archer stretched out his legs. He'd put his feet up on the bed a while ago, about the time he decided he was done working—for the rest of his trip. "And if you'd asked me, I would have advised you against it."

"Why the hell would you do that? Helping clients connect with venture capitalists is a part of our service."

"Yes, isn't it?" He laughed, a little mockingly. "Except I know how Quinntillion operates. You'll see what I mean when you get their term sheet." During the call, Ted's attorney, Dietrich Metzer—who looked and sounded like a nerdy Swiss banker but who was in reality a rapacious, soulless vampire—had said almost nothing. Archer knew that was pure deception. He'd worked at Quinntillion when he was a teenager, and had seen in person how coldly Metzer would cut someone out of their life's work if it led to a bigger payout for Quinntillion.

"They're going to elevate Brightball from marginal start-up to the leading innovator in optical technology."

"Yeah, and in the process they're going to eat away at Bill's control." Some inventors were good with that. They started a company, got it running, sold out, and took their payout to start something newer and more exciting. But Bill lived and breathed Brightball. Archer didn't think he'd want to cede control to Quinntillion or anyone else.

This time Jack's sigh was exasperated. "But that's why we have you, Archer, to look out for Bill's rights. He needs the money, you know how to protect him from Quinntillion's more outrageous demands, everyone will be happy. Why are you acting like I pissed in your coffee?"

He put back his head and stared out the window. Natalie's house lay directly on the other side of that hill. *I don't like lawyers,* echoed her voice in his mind. At the moment, he didn't like lawyers, either, beginning with Jack Harper.

"Jack, did you bring me on just to get business with Quinntillion?"

His boss chuckled. "It didn't hurt, being Ted Quinn's son."

All right; fair enough. He'd suspected as much, although no one at Harper Millman had ever brought up his father. But saying it out in the open had a strangely freeing effect on Archer's thoughts. The vague discontent he'd felt for the last few months suddenly crystalized, and what he wanted became clear.

"You should have done more diligence." Archer sat up and flipped his notebook closed. "If you had, you would have known that this was the first time in six years I've spoken to my father, about business or anything else." If Jack had asked, Archer would also have told him that he'd never try to steer a client toward a deal with Quinntillion, and that he'd regard any such deal as if it had been made by a hostile firm. Not that it mattered now. "I assume you've already talked to Bill about this conflict, and he's still willing to have me working on this?"

"Absolutely!"

"Then do me one favor from here on: no more bullshit surprises, okay?"

"Fine."

"I also want to form my own tech practice within the firm," Archer went on. "Duke Austen has some big ideas in the works. I want to take Elle Williams and create a dedicated team to bring them out. Some of these ideas will generate work for years to come, and I need more than spotty time from an ever-changing variety of associates."

"A tech practice?" Jack sounded doubtful. "I'd have

to run it by the other partners . . ."

"Do that," said Archer, his gaze moving to the hill outside his window. Natalie was probably getting ready for bed by now. Coming to England had been an awesome idea, even if it led to him working with his father. "But if he doesn't approve, I'll be leaving the firm. And Duke Austen will come with me."

"Whoa," exclaimed Jack. "That's blackmail!"

That's the Quinn way, Archer thought. "Not really. Just bald facts. Let me know when I get back to Boston."

"I'm sure we can work out a plan that will suit everyone," Jack began, but Archer was done.

"I have to go, Jack. Good talking to you." He hung up the phone and checked his watch. It was too late to go back to Primrose Cottage, so he went to the unofficial hotel bar, the back patio. Piers Prescott walked by, headed to the pool with a towel over his shoulder.

"Making up for missing the drunken shooting party this morning?" Piers nodded at Archer's glass of scotch.

He took a swallow. "Nope. Celebrating telling off my boss."

Piers's eyebrows shot up. "Why?"

"For manipulating me into working with my father."

"Manipulating?" Piers frowned. "What the hell?"

Archer drank some more scotch, feeling better and better. "You know my father; he's all his reputation cracks him up to be. I haven't spoken to him in years. But tonight, my boss admitted he hired me partly to get business from dear old Ted, which he's just done—and I have to work on the deal. So I told him to go fuck himself."

"Literally?" There was surprise, but also a tinge of envy in the other man's voice.

"More figuratively." Archer imagined Jack Harper's face during their conversation. "But he got my meaning."

Piers Prescott stared at him with a very odd expression.

Archer grinned. "If you're wondering, it feels fantastic."

"Right," murmured Piers.

"Archer!" He turned to see Duke striding across the patio. "More trouble with the magazine deal."

Of course there was. Archer didn't even care this time. He felt like nailing someone's hide to the wall, and a sleazy tabloid hack was as good a choice as any. He thunked his glass down on the bar. "Then let's go crucify the bastard."

CHAPTER NINE

Archer slept late the next morning. After dealing with more outrage from the magazine lawyers—this time over photos of the groom and groomsmen aiming rifles at a cowering paparazzo—he'd had another scotch. When he woke, the sky was dark gray and thunder rumbled in the distance. Normally he would have opened his laptop and spent the morning working; half the wedding party had come home drunk from the bachelor and bachelorette parties the previous night, and the hotel was fairly quiet. But today he pulled on his sneakers and went for a run, finally feeling like a weight had lifted off him. And as he ran, he made a list.

First, he had been working too hard. It hadn't been a lie when he told Natalie he had no time to meet anyone. Now, however, he had greater motivation than ever to delegate more work, especially work related to Brightball's new investor.

Second, he did want to have his own specialty practice. It was good to be in a firm, with guys like Tom available when his clients needed something extra, but Archer wanted more independence. Having a client like

Duke Austen gave him leverage, and he was ready to use it.

And third, he was going to use his greater autonomy and increased delegation to find more free time. Because he had met someone now, and he was ready to blow off work for her. The avalanche had tumbled him head over heels until he had no idea which way was up anymore. The only thing he knew was that he wanted to know everything about her, every little thing that made her laugh or frown or roll her eyes. He wanted to perfect the art of making her cheeks flush pink and her voice go throaty and he wanted to make her come in his arms. He had two more days here, and he meant to spend both of them with her.

That last line of thought quickened his steps until he was almost flying up the gravel path. He took the stairs two at a time, pausing only for a group of women heading down. The bride was in the center of them, glowing with delight. The wedding was tomorrow, he realized, and when Jane caught his eye he gave her a big grin. *Thank you a hundred thousand times for inviting me,* he silently told her. He headed to his room, took a quick shower, and changed. Then he grabbed his key without a second glance at his laptop or phone. Time to see what delicious something he would get to lick off Natalie's skin today.

He went out the back of the house, only to almost run into the wedding planner and hotel owner, who seemed to be having an argument.

"It's completely blown," Arwen Kilpatrick was saying furiously. "Dead. Who knows how long it's been out, and now everything is spoiled because *of course* it would be hot these last few days—"

"But it was only one of four," Harry Compton countered. "It can't be that bad, darling."

"Harry, we have *no dessert!* Not even a bride cake!"

Archer, already starting to detour around them, slowed. No dessert? That sounded intrinsically bad, but her voice was frantic, almost shrill with despair. He tried to think what was planned for today that could have caused a lack of dessert to be a major problem . . .

Oh, right. The formal rehearsal dinner. He hesitated a moment, then turned around.

"Excuse me," he said to the arguing couple.

The hotelier immediately stepped in front of Arwen. "How can I help you?"

"I might be able to help you," he said, watching the wedding planner. "It sounds like there was an equipment malfunction in the kitchen."

"Everything is under control," Compton tried to say but Arwen was having none of that.

"One of our refrigerators died, Mr. Quinn." She drew herself up and managed a smile that was remarkably poised. "But don't worry, I still have almost seven hours to find dessert for nearly a hundred people. I've had worse problems."

"And I have a suggestion." Archer thought of Natalie's wine cooler, filled with barely tasted cakes and pies. "Your neighbor is a chef, writing a cookbook. I know she's been baking desserts for at least a week now. I've tasted some of them and everything is otherworldly."

Arwen's smile slipped a bit. "I'm sure they are, but my desserts came from a top bakery in London."

"She's the deputy chef at Cuisine du Jude, in Wellesley, Massachusetts." Archer was betting a celebrity wedding planner from New York City would have heard of it. If Jack Harper had trouble getting reservations there, it was exclusive and excellent.

And sure enough, Arwen's eyes went wide. "Oh my God," she breathed, turning to Harry Compton. "The most perfect date night restaurant in America! This might work."

Compton looked disconcerted. "A chef? No, the only neighbor is Amaryllis Sonnier, the artist. She's not even here; she spends every summer in Portugal."

"And she's lent her house to Natalie, who has a walk-in wine cooler filled with cakes."

"Cuisine du Jude is exquisite," Arwen babbled. "I ate there last summer to check it out for a client. *Exquisite.* If she can cook half as well as Judith Corcoran . . ."

"Natalie is her daughter." Archer grinned.

Arwen looked at Compton, who shrugged. "I have to give it a shot," she said. "Mr. Quinn, I take it you'll introduce me?"

"I was on my way over there now."

"If this works, I will kiss you," declared Arwen, falling in step beside him. Archer just saw the scowl that crossed Compton's face before he, too, set off through the garden toward Primrose Cottage with them.

Natalie noticed when Archer didn't come down to her cottage the next morning. She told herself it was because of the rain, but then the clouds blew away and still the patio was empty, save for Oliver stretched out on the table where Archer usually worked. Natalie tried not to scowl at the cat. It wasn't his fault Archer hadn't come.

She hoped it wasn't her fault.

The day they'd spent together had been . . . well, pretty nearly perfect. He was funny. He was considerate. He was thoughtful. He bought really good wine for a picnic on the grass. His kisses made her feel like a goddess, and his hands made her think pornographic thoughts. The attraction between them might be roaring along at a breakneck pace, but as Archer said yesterday, she didn't feel like stopping it.

But then where was he?

No. She refused to make herself crazy wondering why he wasn't there. He was a grown man and had things to do. Just because he'd kissed her senseless ... several times ... didn't mean anything. It was pure coincidence that he hadn't shown up after they made out like horny teenagers and then had a daylong date. No, she was a mature, independent woman who would not torture herself trying to understand the mind of any man. She spread out her notes on cookies, trying to decide where to start, and told herself to concentrate on her own work.

It didn't happen. Today, for the first time, she didn't feel like baking. Not even her go-to classic chocolate chip recipe was enticing, nor her scribbled suggestions about oats and nuts and dried fruits. She flicked through the pages, unable to decide, then took out the handwritten recipe for chocolate pudding cake. It did sound good, and Archer had dared her to make it ...

In a huff, she went out onto the patio and dropped into the chair, pushing her legs out straight in front of her. She tipped her head back, letting the sun warm her face. Oliver got to his feet and stretched, then walked across the table and climbed into her lap, purring hard. Natalie ran one hand down his back, smiling up at the sky. At least one male still wanted to get on top of her.

"Maybe I ought to take today off, too," she said to the cat. "I could walk back to town and look in the shops." Such few shops as were in town. "Do you need any kitty toys, Oliver?" His big paws, darker than the rest of him, flexed against her knee. "I don't even know what toys cats like."

"Jingle bells," said Archer from somewhere behind her. "And feathers. At least that's what my mother's cat likes."

Natalie started, and Oliver jumped off her lap with an offended meow. "Oh, hi," she said stupidly, feeling her face turn red. She got up, brushing the cat fur from her skirt.

"Good morning." His eyes warmed as he smiled. She could only smile back like an idiot as his gaze flicked up and down, hot and brazen. "I have a question to ask— actually a tremendous favor—but before I ask, I want you to know it's totally fine if you say no."

"Uh-oh." She tried to laugh even as her heart stuttered ridiculously. "That sounds ominous."

"No, it's just . . ." He hesitated. "I know you're not a fan of the wedding chaos, but the bride and groom are actually really decent people. There's been a malfunction in the kitchen with one of the refrigerators . . ."

The smile slid off her face. "Okay," she said tonelessly when Archer paused again.

He ran one hand over his head, ruffling his hair and raising the wave. "One of the refrigerators died, all the desserts for tonight's rehearsal dinner went bad, and the wedding planner—also a nice person—is in a bind. I know you have a bunch of cakes in the cooler, and I thought maybe you would be willing to help her out."

So he hadn't come down today because he'd been busy chatting with the wedding planner. And he hadn't said one word about yesterday, or asked how she was, or made any sign there was anything at all between them. He wanted her to bail out the same wedding party that had clogged the road, ruined her peace and quiet, and led to random people getting naked on her patio. How did a woman respond to that?

Archer obviously realized he'd gone wrong. "Shit. You'd never know I talk to people for a living. Well—will you just meet her for a minute? I swear to God if you don't want to do it, you don't have to, and I'll send her back up to the hotel."

Natalie lifted one shoulder. "Fine."

He gave her a reassuring smile and loped back out of the garden. He'd obviously brought the wedding planner with him—taking things a bit for granted, she thought sourly. But when he came back a moment later, there were two people with him, a woman with thick bangs cut in her shiny dark hair and a tall man with sharply angular features that managed to be handsome despite being so pronounced.

"Thank you," declared the woman fervently before anyone else could speak. She rushed forward, hand outstretched. "Arwen Kilpatrick. I'm thrilled to meet you—your mother is a visionary and a genius. What she does at Cuisine du Jude is simply amazing."

This made Natalie smile. She shook the woman's hand. "She is. I'm Natalie Corcoran."

The tall man also put out his hand. "Harry Compton," he said in crisp English tones. "I own Brampton House."

She shook his hand, too, although with less enthusiasm. He was responsible for all the traffic on the road, after all. "Hi."

"I hope Archer explained what happened. One of my refrigerators died sometime overnight and everything spoiled—ten cakes from one of the best bakeries in London. The buttercream is in puddles." Arwen took a deep breath. "If you could help in any way, I would be prostrate with gratitude. Money is no object, either. I am desperate, and Archer said he thought he'd died and gone to heaven when he tasted your baking." A glimmer of a smile crossed her face. "I expect Judith Corcoran's daughter must have milk and honey in her veins."

Natalie's reserve was thawing. "Not quite." She glanced at Archer, who looked guarded but hopeful. She remembered it was his client getting married; saving the day would be as much a win for him as it would be for Arwen. "Before you write a blank check, why don't you taste? I do have a bunch of cakes in the cooler, but they may not be what you want."

"*Cake* is what I want," said Arwen. Mr. Compton choked on a laugh.

"I made these this week, but they've all been sampled," Natalie warned as she led the way to the cooler. She hit the switch for the lights and pulled out a tray of chocolate cakes, all missing one thin wedge. "I couldn't bear to throw them out yet. What's your pleasure—chocolate?"

"They all look divine."

No baker could fail to respond to the look of greedy joy on Arwen's face. Natalie turned to Archer. "Would you mind getting some plates and forks?"

They tasted milk chocolate, dark chocolate, and chocolate with cherry filling. Natalie went deeper into the cooler and got out the vanilla cakes, some with coconut, some with strawberries, and one with marbled chocolate and cream cheese frosting. These were almost frozen, but came to freshness in a few minutes when cut into half-inch slices.

"Oh my God, I can die happy right now," moaned Arwen, taking another tiny bite.

"I still have lemon cake and two strawberry tortes," Natalie offered.

Arwen shook her head and put down her plate. "I don't need to taste any more. I want the lot; will you sell them to me?"

"All right." She thought the woman would hug her. "And please give a credit to Cuisine du Jude, and maybe mention there's a forthcoming cookbook with all these recipes."

Arwen laughed. "Done! You have saved my skin. I'll send a van down to pick them all up at five o'clock; is that okay? If the Next Gordon Ramsey squawks about giving me a refrigerator then, I will kill him with my bare hands."

"Which one will be the bride's cake, darling?" Harry Compton has mostly focused on tasting, but now he reached out—to Natalie's surprise—and smoothed away a stray bit of frosting from Arwen's mouth.

The wedding planner seemed to tilt in his direction as his thumb lingered on her lip, then caught herself. She sighed. "I can't worry about that. We'll just have to do without." She caught Natalie's raised eyebrows. "I had a special cake for the bride and groom's table, covered with fondant and real flowers. It's in the waste bin now."

"I could make one of those," Natalie heard herself say. "It would be tight on time, but I could probably do it . . ."

Arwen stared at her, perfectly still. "I would give you my firstborn baby if you could replace that cake."

"No thank you," said Natalie wryly. "I might need

some help, though . . ."

"At your service." Archer winked at her. It was the first time he'd spoken since she brought out the coconut cake. "If you think I'll do."

Slowly, she smiled. "Let's give it a try."

Arwen and Mr. Compton left, promising to send the van and anything she needed from the caterer's supplies up at the hotel. Archer waved good-bye from the kitchen door, then closed it.

Natalie smiled, tucking up her hair. "Ready to be my slave?"

He caught her around the waist and kissed her, hot and intense and dizzying. "Yes," he said in a rough voice. "But first we have to bake a cake."

She toyed with a button on his shirt. "I missed you this morning." It just popped out before she could tell her brain not to admit it.

"I missed you too. Stupid fucking work kept me up last night." He backed her up against the pantry door and kissed her again. Her knees went weak and she clung to his neck, reveling in the weight of his body pressing hers hard against the wood. His hands ran down her waist, over her hips, and back up. She felt high as a kite, feverishly hot and giddy with excitement. He missed her. "You taste like coconut," he breathed, flattening his hand on the small of her back. "I love coconut."

"Better than chocolate?" She tugged his head back so she could run her tongue down his neck. He growled and leaned more heavily against her. Natalie shifted, moving her hips against his magnificent erection. How they were going to bake a cake now was beyond her.

"Whatever you taste like is my favorite." His mouth returned to hers, his tongue plunging deep, and Natalie forgot about cakes of any flavor.

"Okay." When he finally lifted his head and pressed his forehead to hers, his heart thundered against her palm, spread on his chest to hold his shirt. "Okay. How long does it take to make a cake?"

"A while . . ." Almost against her will, she started to tick through the steps in her mind. "Four to five hours, I think."

He exhaled. "Then this will have to wait." His hand, cupped around her butt, squeezed, and he slowly let her go. "Ready to bake?"

She was ready to tear off her clothes and throw caution to the wind, along with her panties. Hell, they probably wouldn't be the first people to have sex on these counters. But she had promised Arwen she would make the damn cake, and Archer had said only *wait,* meaning they were going to pick back up where they left off, so she let him back away and reached for her apron. "If we must."

For someone who claimed not to cook, Archer was at home in the kitchen. He rolled up his sleeves and followed her every direction. Thankfully Natalie had thrown a pair of square pans into the many boxes of baking supplies she'd shipped from home, so she set him to lining those with parchment and buttering everything. She swept aside all the cookie notes and busied herself with butter, sugar, and eggs as she mentally planned the cake. She still had fresh strawberries in the refrigerator, and a half-gallon of thick English cream to make a filling between the layers. There was no fondant in the kitchen, but she could make a rich buttercream frosting and slick it as smooth as glass. A quick piping of a lacy pattern with tinted frosting would finish the cake, and if Arwen had clean fresh flowers at Brampton House, she could add a few at the last moment.

Natalie had spent many hours baking with her mother, where naturally she fell into the junior role. Now that she was shoulder to shoulder with Archer, though, she realized how much she'd changed in the six weeks she'd spent in England. It felt right to be in charge, to direct every step of the creation—*her* creation, not a copy of her mother's work. Judy didn't even do wedding cakes, but Natalie was making one up on the fly. And it was fun.

When Archer dropped an egg on the floor and swore, she only laughed. When she caught him licking the empty bowl while she spread batter into the waiting pans, she flicked flour at him. When he lobbed a dollop of batter back at her and it landed on her cheek, she protested until he pinned her against the dishwasher and licked it off with soft, gentle kisses. She'd barely set the timer for the cakes before he lifted her to sit on the counter and went back to kissing her. Natalie closed her eyes to the messy kitchen and curled her legs around his waist to hold him closer.

"When are you going home?" he whispered some time later, nuzzling her ear.

"Hmm?" She had her hand inside his unbuttoned shirt, mesmerized by the feel of his skin, so hot and firm against her fingers.

"Home." He nipped her earlobe. "To Boston."

Home to Boston. To her parents. To the Jude. To her brother, and the feud still simmering between them. Her fingers slowed to a stop.

"I'm leaving on Sunday," Archer went on. "But I want to see you again—soon, and often. How much more cookbook do you have to write?"

Only quick breads and biscuits, she realized. She'd gone through meats and seafood, vegetables, salads, pasta, and now dessert. Amaryllis would be coming home in a month, putting an end to her stay anyway. Soon she'd have to pack up her pans, and her pride, and go back to face her family. "I don't know when I'm going home," she murmured.

Archer pulled back, finally picking up her mood change. He took her face in his hands and studied her. "Why not?"

"I guess I'm not looking forward to it."

He just waited. Natalie sighed, letting her head tilt into his hand, so warm and strong and comforting. She'd liked his hands from the start. "I left because I lost my temper and poured soup on my brother, in front of a restaurant full of people. I haven't been there since, because . . . Well, because I acted like a crazy bitch and I know it."

"Do you want to go back?"

She blinked. "I do! Of course I do!" Although . . . Did she? Now she was used to being in charge of the kitchen. If her dad was recovering, her mother would come back to Cuisine du Jude, and as much as Natalie loved cooking with her mother . . . "I think I do."

Archer was quiet for a minute. Inanely, Natalie felt grateful; the men in her family were used to filling any silence, overriding any uncertainty, always ready with their advice whether welcome or not. "You know," he finally said, "if you wanted to open your own place, I know some investors . . ."

"My own place!" She scoffed. "What would I do with my own place?" Besides desserts and breads. She may have bragged about being able to disembowel a whole turkey, but her favorite thing was baking, from crackers and scones to cookies and—as of today—wedding cake.

Archer lifted one shoulder. "If you go into wedding

cakes, Arwen would probably throw a ton of business your way. She offered you her firstborn child, after all."

Natalie laughed, and then she thought about it. A bakery? Without effort, plans started sprouting in her mind. It would get her away from Paul, yet offer the brand expansion he wanted. She would have her own kitchen, make her own menu, try her own experiments, but with ties to the Jude. And it would work well with her cookbook, provided she could find a publisher. Those were *her* recipes, no longer her mother's. The cookbook had begun as a face-saving project, but had gradually become something she really cared about. The fact that it was now associated with meeting Archer only made it better.

"You could think about it." Archer gave her a slight smile. "I may be useless in the kitchen, but I do know how to form a company."

She wound her arms around his neck. "You are definitely not useless in the kitchen."

While the cakes cooled, she set him to cutting the strawberries into thin slices so she could make the whipped cream filling, flavored with framboise and vanilla. Archer leaned his head over the mixer and inhaled deeply, sighing in pleasure. "This has been the best damn vacation of all time."

She laughed. "And you spent most of it working on the patio!"

He fed her a heart-shaped strawberry slice. "That should tell you how awesome the other parts have been, to outweigh thirty-five hours of work."

The afternoon sped by. As she split the cakes and filled them, they talked about what would be involved in setting up a Cuisine du Jude bakery, legally. Archer told her it could be structured so that she was the head of the bakery division and somewhat independent of Paul. Thinking of herself as head of a business made Natalie shake her head, but now the idea had grown roots. As she spread the buttercream over the cake, stacking the layers and smoothing away loose crumbs, the bakery took shape in her mind.

The van arrived while she was piping the last few swirls of pale violet icing, and she felt a thrill of pride as the caterers boxed up her work and carried it away almost reverently. Archer caught her behind the kitchen door as the caterers loaded the van. "I'd better go back and shower," he said. There was flour in his hair and he had buttercream all over his shirt. "I'm coming back later."

Natalie slid her hands around his waist. "I thought I'd go oversee the dessert course. Just in the kitchen. Maybe you can walk me home."

"You bet," he growled, and kissed her hard before following the caterers.

A loopy grin stuck to her face, she watched him go, waving once as he leaned out the window and blew her a kiss. The van pulled away, and she went back into the house to clean up, both herself and her kitchen.

But she stood over the batter-spotted counter and reached for her phone instead. She tapped on her brother's contact, and their last round of texts came up on the screen.

I don't think you can replicate what Mom & Dad do in LA or Chicago, she'd said.

Not trying to replicate, Nat. Build and grow, Paul had replied.

How can you build a brand without doing more of the same? she'd asked.

More of similar, not the same, was his answer.

Two days after that exchange she'd poured soup on him.

It would be almost lunchtime in Boston. Paul was probably at the restaurant. She could picture him walking through the dining room making sure everything was set, opening umbrellas on the dining patio if the weather was nice, helping restock the bar or even clean up a mess in the kitchen. He was there as much as she was, because he loved the Jude as much as she did—in slightly different ways, but no less dearly. She took a deep breath and typed out a new text. *What would you think of a Jude bakery location?* For a moment her finger hovered over the Send button, then she resolutely tapped it. It was the first thing she'd said to her brother in two months. Maybe she should have spoken to her parents first. Maybe she should have slept on it. Maybe—

The phone buzzed in her hand. *Possibility. Where?*

Boston area, she typed back. *Run by me.*

She almost held her breath, waiting to see what he would say to that last bit. Their mother had ceded most business control to their father, but Natalie wasn't willing to do the same with her brother. If she started a bakery, it would have to be her shop, not run at Paul's, or even Dad's, direction.

Only baked goods or serving lunch as well?

She let out a shaky breath. The peace offering had been accepted. *Lunch possible if the Jude will supply meats/soups/etc.*

The next reply came almost at once. *That could work. Discuss when you get back?*

Natalie grinned as she typed *Sure.* Then she quickly texted her mother about the exchange, feeling as if she'd just shed a huge weight. The fight had cast a dark cloud over her whole family. Her parents would be so happy to put an end to it, they'd probably be waiting at the airport with balloons.

She glanced out the window, at the green hill sloping up beyond the garden, hiding Brampton House from her sight. She had her first event tonight—under her own name, not just Cuisine du Jude's—and Archer was going to walk her home. She ran upstairs to shower and change.

CHAPTER TEN

The cocktail hour was well underway when Archer reached the reception. He took a beer and wandered about, restless without Natalie. She was coming up to the house, she'd said; was she here already? It would be rude to leave the party and invade the kitchen, but he had nothing to say to anyone else.

The dinner was a smashing success, as far as he could tell. When the guests sat down in the Gold Saloon, at each place was a small, hand-lettered card announcing that the dessert tonight had been provided by Natalie Corcoran of Cuisine du Jude in Wellesley, Massachusetts. From the murmur of amazement that went around the tables, Archer guessed the restaurant's fame had spread far and wide. He wished Natalie could hear it, then decided he could just tell her about it later. Knowing what was coming made the rest of the meal—excellent otherwise—seem endless. He managed to get through it by chatting with a few programmers at his table, including the amorous Rupert and his girlfriend. They took some good-natured teasing about their romantic activities, which didn't seem to bother either of them in the slightest.

When dessert was finally served, the guests grew a bit quieter. Mr. Delancey opened the doors, and a parade of catering staff wheeled in elegant dessert trolleys. Each held a gleaming tower of fine china plates bearing slices of cake, arranged to showcase the variety of options. And at the end of the train came Natalie, pushing a trolley with the special bridal cake they had made together, now adorned with deep purple roses. Even in a plain black skirt and white shirt, like all the other servers, she was gorgeous. Archer found himself grinning like an idiot as she went past all the other tables to the head one, where Jane and Duke sat with their immediate family. If the expression on Jane's face didn't convince Natalie that she could make it as a bakery owner, nothing would.

The other carts circulated along the tables, offering each diner a choice of cake slices. "Which would you like, sir?" the waiter asked Archer.

"Doesn't matter," he said without taking his eyes off Natalie. "They're all fantastic."

He caught up to her after dinner, as the guests began to filter out. Music started up somewhere for dancing, so he swept her into his arms and spun her around.

"That went better than I thought it would," she said, beaming.

"People were fainting away in ecstasy as they ate." He kissed her. "Do you want to dance or shall we go?"

She smiled and went up on her toes, pressing against him. "Let's go," she whispered.

Archer grabbed her hand and headed for the door, stopping only to snag a bottle of champagne at the bar. Duke Austen, walking by with Jane plastered to his side, saw them. His eyes flicked toward Natalie, then back to

Archer, and he smirked. Archer just raised the bottle in salute and kept going, through the garden, up the hill, toward the stone house with the quaint name, the best Wi-Fi of all time, and plenty of privacy to make love to Natalie all night long.

"Thank you," she said as they walked.

"It was all you. And a success like that deserves a toast." Archer popped the cork and offered her the foaming bottle.

Natalie laughed as she tilted it to her mouth. "True, but I meant for your idea earlier. About the bakery."

"That was all your idea too." He took a drink himself. "But one I selfishly applaud. I'll be first in line when you open."

She kicked off her shoes and scooped them up. "You know, it never occurred to me until you said that. My brother wants to open other restaurants, and I was so focused on preventing that, I never tried to find a compromise that would suit us both. I texted him today and I think he likes the idea too."

"The art of a good deal. Everyone gets something they want." He offered her the bottle again.

"I should probably find a lawyer, huh?"

Archer made a face. "Lawyers suck. You hate them."

"Really?" She tugged him to a stop. "I'm revising that opinion."

He caught her against him. "Don't do that. Just . . . Make an exception."

Her arms went around his neck. "Yeah," she whispered. "You're definitely the exception."

"Natalie." He inhaled deeply as she kissed his throat. "We need to walk faster."

"Why?" She nipped his skin and he shuddered. He was already so hard, he wasn't sure he *could* walk faster, but . . .

"Because otherwise I'm going to throw you to the ground right here and now. So unless you want grass stains on your skirt . . ."

With a peal of laughter she broke away. She took another gulp from the champagne and danced backward out of his reach. The path to Primrose Cottage had never seemed longer as they strode through the damp grass, passing the bottle back and forth. They reached the familiar patio, lit by the glow of the kitchen lights.

Natalie turned to walk backward again, her gaze riveted on him as she unbuttoned her white shirt. His eyes burned as she ripped it off, exposing her lacy pink bra. He barely managed to leave the empty champagne bottle on the table where he'd spent so many hours working before he grabbed her around the waist, lifting her up the steps to the door. With some laughing and a few whispered curses, she fumbled the key out of her skirt pocket and he let them in, almost stepping on Oliver as they crashed into the kitchen and up against the pantry door.

"We seem to have a thing for this door," she gasped as his hands covered her breasts.

"It's the best damn door in the world," he growled.

She tugged on his tie. "Prove it."

Shaking with lust, he ran a hand up her leg. Her skin was bare, all the way up. She wasn't wearing underwear. "Shit," he said hoarsely. "Thank God I didn't know that earlier . . ." She started to laugh, but he ran one fingertip between her legs, probing into the soft, wet folds, then sliding inside her. That made the laugh clog in her throat until she stopped breathing entirely.

He groped in his pocket while she made short work of his belt and zipper. She took the condom from him and he let her; his entire being was focused on the gentle but firm touch of her hands on his cock as she rolled it on. Her skirt was already around her waist and he almost came on the spot as he pushed hard inside her.

Oh *God*. There—this—that was what she'd been craving. Natalie bit down on her lip to keep from moaning out loud, then remembered there was no one within a mile to hear her. "Again," she panted, clinging to his shoulders. Archer laughed even as he cupped his hands beneath her butt so she could hook her legs around his hips. Then he began to move.

She pushed and writhed, seeking the perfect friction between them. His mouth moved ravenously over her, teasing the skin beneath her ear, sucking at the curve of her throat. The champagne and the thrill of the wedding guests' reaction to her cakes had already sent her flying high; now she thought she would literally burst. The door behind her back rattled every time Archer surged into her, sharp and hard and fast enough to make her toes curl and her breath degenerate into ragged gasps as her orgasm built like a tidal wave inside her. Oh God—she wasn't ready—or maybe she was—

"Yes," she cried as he drew it from her, long and sinuous and crackling with electricity. "Oh my *God,* yes." She was out of her head, punch-drunk on the high of good sex. He changed his angle, driving hard and deep, and wrung another aftershock of climax from her as his own hit. He leaned his full weight into her and exhaled a long, low groan, and she tightened her grip on him. Partly because she didn't want to fall, but mostly because she didn't want to let him go.

Ever.

Archer moved against her. "How do you feel about the door now?" he murmured against her throat.

"I love it. I have to get one for my apartment at home."

His shoulders shook in a silent laugh. He raised his head and kissed her, softly and sweetly. "I want to stay the night."

She nodded. There was nothing else to say.

He let her down onto her feet and eased away. Gratefully, Natalie leaned on the counter as he put himself back together. Her legs were shaking and her heart was hammering. She hadn't even known it could be that good. "Oh," she said dazedly, catching sight of the pan she'd left on top of the AGA. "I forgot. I made you something."

Archer peeled off his jacket. "Did you?"

She raised a corner of the tinfoil covering the pan. "You said you wanted to see if I could make it as well as your mom . . ."

He went still in the midst of pulling loose his tie. "Is that—?" His voice was hushed and incredulous.

She nodded, reaching for a spoon. "Chocolate pudding cake." She scooped out a bite and held it up.

"Good Lord in heaven." His eyes rolled upward as he ate. "You made this for me?"

"Who else?" Natalie grinned. "I had just enough time between when you left and when I had to go to Brampton House . . ."

Archer spooned up a second bite and fed it to her. "Now do you see?" he murmured.

Her eyes widened as the light chocolate cake turned silky on her tongue. "Mmm."

"Exactly," he breathed, a moment before he kissed

her. His fingers stole up her back and snapped the clasp on her bra. She pulled it off as he shed his shirt and finally they were skin to skin. "Natalie," he whispered, nibbling her ear. "I think I'm in love."

She blushed. "Because of the cake?"

His mouth quirked. "The cake only made me say it out loud. But you should know this isn't just a hookup for me."

She touched his chin. There was a tiny cleft there she had never noticed before. "Not for me, either."

"If you want rid of me, you'd better say so now."

For a few heartbeats her thoughts raced. "And if I don't?" she asked slowly.

"I'm going to take you upstairs and shag you six ways to Sunday," he said in a surprisingly good—and terribly sexy—British accent.

"Well," she said softly, winding her arms around his neck. "I like your terms. We have a deal, Mr. Quinn."

Natalie awoke to find herself alone in bed, although Archer's presence was all around. His shirt still hung from the top of the door, and his tie was on the bedside table. When she rolled over, she could smell him on the pillow next to hers. For a moment she just wallowed in it, feeling blissed out and mellow. He had indeed shagged her six ways to Sunday: on the bed, in the shower, and once from behind, when she woke up spooned against him while his marvelous hands wandered purposefully over her until she was begging for more. At the memory, she smiled a sleepy, satisfied smile and wondered where he was. His clothes were still here, so he must be as well.

A distant rattle made her eyes fly open, and a muffled curse made her sit up. That came from the kitchen. What on earth . . . ? She got out of bed and pulled on her robe, tying it around her waist.

Sure enough, Archer was in the kitchen. The table was set for two, and he was standing in front of the open refrigerator. A large number of pans were on the AGA and in the sink, and she realized he'd been making breakfast.

"Good morning," she said, her voice scratchy— probably from screaming her head off in ecstasy all night.

He whipped around. Clad only in his suit pants with a dishtowel draped over his shoulder, his hair rumpled and a scruff of whiskers darkening his jaw, he was the sexiest sight she'd ever seen. Something inside her lurched as he smiled his lazy, sly grin. "Good morning."

"You look busy." She motioned to the dishes, the table, the stove.

He looked around at the mess. "I hope I get points for effort. My actual cooking . . . Probably not." He grimaced at the sink, and she leaned over to see two ruined eggs and a handful of blackened toasts.

Helplessly she laughed. "Major points for effort."

"Good. At least I didn't ruin the strawberries." He came around the table and kissed her, first lightly, then wrapping his arms around her and deepening the kiss. "Good morning."

"It is, isn't it?" She could have purred like Oliver as his hands went down her back.

"Today is the wedding," he murmured. "I have to go." She made a soft noise of agreement as his hands found the hem of her short silky robe and eased it upward. "Come with me," he said then.

Her eyes popped open in surprise. "I don't know

anyone in that wedding!"

"You know me." He tipped up her chin and kissed her again, the long, hypnotic kiss that messed with her brain. "Jane and Duke would be happy to have you, and Arwen would probably rearrange every table to get you in, after the way you saved her rehearsal dinner."

"So," she said breathlessly, trying to regain her ability to think. "So. You want me to come with you, like a date?" It felt weird to ask that; usually she went on several official dates with a guy before she slept with him. Not that anything had gone "as usual" with Archer, and so far it was turning out far better than usual.

"No," he said slowly. "I think I'd rather you come with me like a girlfriend."

She jumped. "We've barely known each other a week! We haven't gone out on a regular date . . ."

He grinned, dipping his head to the side in that endearing way he had. "The wedding will be the first. And tonight will be the second. Then there will be a lot more once we get home."

"And we've already had sex," she went on nonsensically.

"Which will also happen again." His eyes darkened as he tugged at the sash of her robe. She couldn't even blush as he pushed it open and ran his hands over her bare skin, making her melt inside. "Right here on the kitchen counter, just as soon as you agree to come to the wedding with me."

"That's unhygienic," she whispered as he backed her up against the counter.

"Hot," he retorted. He scooped up a bit of whipped cream from a nearby bowl and swirled it around her exposed nipple.

Natalie moaned helplessly as the cold cream hit her skin. "Archer . . ."

"Say yes." He bent his head and licked at the cream. "Just to the wedding date for now."

She couldn't move. She was barely keeping her balance. As if he knew, he ran his fingers through the whipped cream and then dragged them down her body, from the notch of her collarbone, down between her breasts, over her belly, right between her legs. "But—but— You asked me to be your girlfriend. You even said the L word."

"I did." With shocking ease, he boosted her to sit on the counter. He tugged the robe off her shoulders and then pushed her knees wide, his face dark and taut with hunger as he looked her over. Natalie stared back in fascination. He yanked over a chair and knelt on it to start licking away the trail of cream he'd painted on her. And as his mouth leisurely moved lower, Natalie gave herself over to his persuasion.

"So, are you thinking about it?" He glanced up as he eased her back.

"What?" Her wits were scattered by the heat of his mouth on her flesh and by the anticipation of what was coming. No one had gone down on her in years and she was taken off guard by how badly she wanted it now— from him.

"The date part." He ran his fingertips lightly up her inner thigh, and she flinched so hard she almost fell over. "And the girlfriend part."

"Exclusive girlfriend?" she asked, not shocked by how ragged and husky her voice was. It was a miracle she could form words at all.

"The one and only."

"I . . . I'm thinking . . ." she said faintly.

His eyes glittered. "Good." His hands spread wide on her thighs and he lowered his head.

She had a hazy thought that if this was some sort of boyfriend audition, he was acing it. His lips were soft, his tongue firm. He held her in place as she rocked and twisted, blown away by the sharp pleasure of his mouth. He seemed to know exactly what to do, backing off just when it grew too intense, alternately gentling or dominating. She forced open her eyes to look in wonder on this man who had learned her so well so fast, and met his scorching gaze head-on. He was watching her, reading her . . . Then he pushed two long fingers inside her and broke her, his mouth pulling on her clit as she came, harder than she'd ever come in her life.

"Still thinking?" he rasped several minutes later, sounding as though he'd just run the marathon.

Dumbly, she shook her head.

"I heard you scream *yes* at least three times."

She smiled, uncaring that she was sprawled on the kitchen counter with traces of whipped cream on her skin. She would never forget this kitchen. "Did I?"

"You did." He pressed a lingering kiss to the inside of her thigh. "Was that your answer?"

With some effort she pushed herself upright. He grinned, looking rumpled and devastatingly sexy. She'd been right about him from the start—guys this *right* didn't walk into a girl's life every day. "Yes—times three."

ABOUT THE AUTHOR

Caroline Linden was born a reader, not a writer. She earned a math degree from Harvard University and wrote computer software before turning to writing fiction. Since then the Boston Red Sox have won the World Series three times, which is not related but still worth mentioning. Her books have been translated into seventeen languages, and have won the NEC Reader's Choice Award, the NJRW Golden Leaf Award, the Daphne du Maurier Award, and RWA's RITA Award.

Visit www.CarolineLinden.com to sign up for notifications about her new books, exclusive bonus content, and a free short story. You can also find her on twitter (@Caro_Linden) or on Facebook (AuthorCarolineLinden).

If you enjoyed this story, please consider posting a review of it online for other readers. Thank you!

Will You Be My Wi-Fi? was originally published as part of the anthology *At the Billionaire's Wedding*, featuring stories from Maya Rodale, Miranda Neville, and Katharine Ashe. If you want to read more about Arwen the harried wedding planner and why she's arguing with Harry Compton; or what's up with Piers Prescott; or what's really going on behind the scenes with Jane and Duke and the problems that beset their wedding, *At the Billionaire's Wedding* is available in print and at major online retailers.

And if you can't get enough of Jane and Duke, check out the Bad Boy Billionaire series by Maya Rodale, which inspired the anthology.

www.ingramcontent.com/pod-product-compliance
Lightning Source LLC
Chambersburg PA
CBHW071004120726
47910CB00004B/1381